INDIANAPOLIS

JASPER
The Gloves Are Off

A Novella

by
A.B. Patterson

Based on the original screenplay by Nathan Hill

FOREWORD

"She had a rack that would've distracted a Catholic priest from
the altar boys"

-A.B. Patterson, "Wankers"

It's the kind of soft pulpy prose with just enough know to guarantee a reader's swift subjection. It still stands up as one hell of a first fuckin' line, but it wasn't the first thing I'd ever read by A.B. Patterson.

If you don't know A.B.'s work, you're about to. I've heard it said the work of A.B. Patterson could be compared to a hybrid of Henry Miller and Ross MacDonald. And for any 2020's Gen Z normies who wandered onto these pages by mistake only to be outraged with entitled claims of "misogyny", declaring this is the work of an old white man, this is where I let you know you're overthinking it—and while we're at it, I'll remind you that in about 16 years, when the world you know flips (every generation does), you'll be earmarked as the uptight set and outdated quicker than last year's men's skinny jeans. So, by that rational consider this book progressive!

You have to remember, back in 2008 when pre-production for *Jasper* started, the world was a different place. No #metoo. And don't get me wrong—Bill Cosby, Harvey Weinstein, those guys can fuck right off. They're rotten to the core. But something's been lost. These days all you have to do is poke your head onto X (the hellscape formerly known as Twitter) and you're gobsmacked by every other word being *toxic masculinity* or *misogyny*. BTW, misogyny (an Ancient Greek word)—the exacerbated term (and misused) for sexism, first became part of popular culture back in the 70s, courtesy of American feminist icon Andrea Dworkin who also aligned herself with right wing zealot Edwin Meese and his legion of anti-pornography conservatives (Now I'm not an expert on feminism, but I'd say that fact alone ought to have gotten Ms. Dworkin's OG feminist card pulled).

When I heard A.B. Patterson had been tapped to novelize Nathan Hill's cult-favorite film, *Jasper,* I knew it was a perfect fit. Two Aussies working in different mediums. Two creatives who always manage to push the envelope. Each with a similar brand of mischievous humor.

A veteran of the Aussie mean streets, A.B. Patterson is a retired police detective who cut his teeth writing for the American pulps. He's been a long-time contributor to the likes of *The EconoClash Review, Pulp Modern,* and *Switchblade.* One thing you can always count on when it comes to A.B.'s work is that wherever the line is, he's going to roll right over it. His fiction is not for the faint of heart. He just can't help himself. His work would've been a tough sell back in 1976, let alone now in the midst of the 2020s Puritanical revival. But no matter how serious or crude the subject matter, his work is never without humor.

If you've never seen Nathan Hill's 2011 private eye-thriller *Jasper,* reading this will be a real treat. And if you have, this book will make you want to watch it again. Written, directed, and starring the Aussie triple threat Nathan Hill, Jasper Clay is a seductive super-sleuth that packs a paunch. (that's right, Jasper lets it all hang out) It's a film that's self-aware, always winking at the audience; dripping with subtext and colorful humor. Jasper is a one-last-job-private-dick that shags a half dozen women in about 48 hours. Male fantasy? Sure, but Jasper's no 007 down under, He's not without his foibles. That's part of what makes *Jasper* so much fun: Nathan Hill is in on the joke. The film, now an underground classic, was the first film in Australia to be shot on a Canon 5D. According to Hill, it was about a three-year journey, and rounds out a formidable list of talent including Sally Greenwood, Catherine Mack, Sarah Howette, and featuring music from *Ninja Academy*—whom Hill discovered at the Viper Room while visiting L.A.

So what you're about to read is the creative amalgamation of an actor-writer-director who unabashedly creates his own independent content while simultaneously infiltrating the Australian cinema and TV industry; and a real-life Sydney private eye and former police detective. It's not your average team-up, but then again, Jasper Clay isn't your average private detective. It's one final case, a mob run town, a whole lot of shagging, and the missing son of a whore.

This isn't high literature, so get off your fuckin' high horse, and if you're an effete Brooklyn lit critic with a designer label MFA, more tattoos than Bieber, and a two million dollar one-bedroom in Williamsburg…Then what the fuck's got you slumming with your cheeky edgelord uncle, Uncle B?

—Scotch Rutherford
author of *The Roach King of Paradise*

A.B. Patterson and Nathan Hill

CHAPTER 1

A hell of a lot of pussy. That's the upside of being a private investigator. This job has got me more pussy than a Beijing barbecue, believe me. Maybe PI should stand for "pussy inquisitor" instead.

But there's a sour side to match the sweet. The yin and yang of life. Yep, dealing with the lowlifes, arguing to get paid, getting a belting every now and then. And none of this cushy stuff like paid holidays, sick leave, or a pension fund.

So, here I was this afternoon having finally decided to pack it all in. I wasn't sure what I'd do moving on, and it wasn't the first time I'd spat the dummy and decided to throw it away. But I'd never taken that final step to packing up the office. Hence, today was different.

I took another swig on the bottle of whiskey that habitually resided in my bottom desk drawer. That tasted good. When doesn't it? That was rhetorical. If you're the sort of person who can even contemplate a time it doesn't, then you are not my type. Then I lit a small cigar. That tasted damned fine, too. I slowly puffed on it for a few minutes as I looked around my decrepit office. More whiskey. Beautiful.

I continued putting the desk-top items into the cardboard filing box: pen holder, notepads, ashtray. I picked up the framed photo that had brightened up my desk for years. Audrey had brightened up a long weekend some years back. Most of it was spent horizontal, but Audrey insisted that she spent so many hours naked wrapped around a pole that a weekend naked on her back was just what the doctor ordered. Any doctor would have been horrified at what followed. Yep, in my books you go hard or you go home.

I gazed at Audrey, naked but for a G-string with a rack that would knock the pyramids off the list of wonders. She'd even signed it for me, "Thank you, lover boy. Audrey XOXO".

I'm not usually one to keep photos around, but that was so memorable. I laid Audrey's image in the box.

Last job was the top drawer. I lifted out my 9mm Beretta and clipped it on my belt. Two boxes of shells went into the packing box.

Another couple of swigs from the bottle. Angel's breath.

I ran my hand around the drawer to make sure it was empty and came out with a pair of skimpy, magenta lace knickers. I smiled to myself as I reminisced. Hell, I could even smell her still.

In my books, souvenirs are cool as long as you knew the lady concerned. You don't have to remember their name, and whilst I could picture the former owner of this aromatic garment in vivid detail, spreadeagled on this very desk as it happened, I couldn't pick her name. But I could claim to have known the lady. Not that I left her a lady. In fact, she hadn't been a lady beforehand either. But she'd been a client who couldn't pay her bill, at least not in any form of payment recognised by the tax office. After a combined five orgasms, that incidentally ruined my desk blotter, she peeled off moist patches of blotting paper from her arse cheeks and left them next to her knickers. With that she was gone. So, my payment ended up being two great shags and the souvenired underwear.

No, knicker souvenirs are only a problem when you've purloined them from a clothesline. I actually caught a snowdropper in the act once, in a neighbour's back yard. I kicked him so hard in his nuts that I reckon he would have got away with comfortably wearing women's knickers from that day on. Filthy fucking pervert.

Talking of payment in kind, it had been a regular feature of my PI life. Something about me attracted the young single mummies needing a gumshoe to track down the deadshit fathers of their kids, an address to facilitate getting some child support from the arseholes. And then not able to afford a PI's cash rates. Yeah, I was always open to negotiation, at least with the ladies. So, job done and deadshit located, I'd get laid. But the kids usually started getting child support, so it's like I'm providing a sort of public benefit, really. Who knew Jasper Clay's beef bayonet was capable of performing such community service? Mind you, I guess I won't be getting a mention in the Australia Day's honours list.

When I finished the cigar, I stubbed it out in a dead pot plant on the windowsill. I swigged from the bottle, put the cap back on it, and stuck it in the box with my meagre professional possessions. I picked up the box—not much to show for the years, really—and looked around one last time. Not much to show, except for memories that the Marquis de Sade would have envied. Priceless. I closed the door behind me and headed for the stairs.

The silence in the empty building was shattered by my office phone ringing.

"Fuck!" I yelled at the walls. To answer or not to answer. Could be the miserable, tight-arsed landlord chasing rent. That wanker made Shylock look like a philanthropist. Or it could be a client wanting to pay an outstanding bill. Hope springs eternal. I stepped back into the office, putting the box down.

I picked up the phone. "Hello?"

It was a frantic-sounding female, not Shylock. "Mister Clay, I need your help, please." The underlying huskiness of her voice wasn't entirely lost in the desperation. There was still plenty of syrup in that sultry siren's call.

"Sorry, lady, I'm getting out of the business."

"But, pleeeeease, Mister Clay." She started crying.

There was a note to her plaintive voice that flickered somewhere in my booze-soaked recesses, some vague familiarity. Or maybe I was imagining things. I often do. I'd eaten so much syrup from seductresses over the years it was hard to tell any longer.

"Like I said, lady, I'm retiring."

Her sobbing turned into a breakdown, from the sound coming down the line. I opened the whiskey bottle and had a gulp as I held the phone receiver away from my ear. I could hear "please" repeatedly amongst the tears.

I put the phone back to my ear. "Lady, please calm down. What is the problem?"

She calmed immediately, presumably guessing she had an opening. The dames normally have that effect on me. Well, I could have worse flaws—I could be a fucking politician or a property developer. Though not much distinction there, to be frank.

"My little boy has been taken."

"Darling, I think that's a matter for the police."

"No, I can't. Please come round and I'll explain."

Again, my memory recesses sparked. But I couldn't place it.

"Okay, I'll come and talk, but I'm not saying I'll take on the job."

"Oh, thank you, Mister Clay. Thank you."

"What's the address?"

I scribbled it and her name, Courtney, on a notepad as she spoke. The name didn't ring a bell. But we've already established I'm not the best on the ladies' names.

"I'll be there a bit later this evening." Yes, I succumbed to a siren's call again. I could see why, back in the day, Odysseus tied himself to the ship's mast as they cruised past the sirens on the rocks. Well, big old Odysseus obviously did rather better on the self-discipline front than Jasper Clay. Any time I've been tied up it was the opposite of trying to avoid sex, if you get my drift.

I hung up. I looked at the phone. I pulled the plug from the wall socket and dumped the bloody thing in my box. I wouldn't get waylaid from my retirement path again.

Jasper Clay, I thought to myself, you deserve a retirement drink. Time for a quick visit to my favourite little bar around the corner, along with my favourite little barmaid, Kinky Krissy.

CHAPTER 2

After throwing the box of desk detritus, Audrey's photo excepted from that description, oh and the knickers, in the boot of the car, I walked around the corner to The Kavern and slipped in the front door. I adjusted my eyes to the semi-nocturnal interior of the tiny wine bar. Krissy liked dark. Liked it hard and wet, too. The bar was so deserted I wondered if I'd have to serve myself.

I plonked myself on my usual bar stool and was just lighting a smoke when Krissy walked in from the back room. As usual, her Spandex low-cut top, black today, was losing the struggle against her magnificent breasts. It was a struggle I unfailingly lost, too, but always with a smile on my face. Well, I'm a gracious loser, aren't I.

Krissy sashayed over, headlights definitely in front. Was that high beam I detected? And why the hell shouldn't she show off her assets? The rich and powerful wankers that run our sordid society flash their assets every day and in every form of media. Krissy, with a heart of gold, had had a shit childhood and was now just trying to hold an adult life together. She used whatever edge she could get. I respect anyone like Krissy.

I grinned at her as she slunk towards me. Her rack beat her elbows to rest on the mahogany bar.

"I was beginning to think this joint had turned self-service."

"A girl's got to split the whisker every now and then."

"Hello, Krissy, you gorgeous girl."

"What can I get you, handsome?"

"Krissy, baby, that's an eternally loaded question."

She ran her tongue across her teeth under her top lip. I felt some movement. I'm only human.

"Black Label on the rocks, baby."

"Ah, the usual then. And any other 'usuals' you might want, sweet Jasper?"

More movement. I groaned. "Oh, Krissy. How tempting, but I've got a client to see."

She poured me a generous glass and then took the fresh cigarette that I was just about to light from my hand.

"I hadn't finished with that, gorgeous."

"Ha ha, you haven't started it." She leant over as I struck my lighter. She inhaled deeply and looked me in the eye. Oh, trouble cometh.

"I haven't seen you in a while, honey."

"Yeah, been busy. And been drinking in better places lately."

She pouted in mock outrage. "Ouch! Bite me, Jasper. Who's been treating you better than old Krissy?"

I laughed. I loved this girl. Without the romantic bit, you understand.

She picked up the whiskey bottle. "Jasper, you stud."

"No, babe, I really do have a client to see. One last one before I retire from the gumshoe life."

"It's okay, darling Jasper, it's on me." She heaved her bosom closer across the bar. "Retiring?"

I nodded at her. "Yep, had enough."

"So, before you rush off to your last client and leave poor Krissy all lonely, do you want the house special to go with that drink? You sure look like you could use one."

I really am a hopeless prick. Well, if you were at eye level with Krissy's assets, and assuming you're straight, you'd be hopeless, too. In fact, I would be surprised if those magnetic mammaries couldn't convert a few of the other team.

She rubbed her fingers through my hair. My capitulation was faster than the fall of Singapore.

"Well, you know what? A house special sounds bang on right now. But this one last client ..."

"But you retiring or not?"

"Yes, but I've got a feeling about this last one. Got the call as I was packing up my office."

She grinned and stroked my face. Her voice dropped an octave and went all husky. "I've got a feeling, too, you hunky beast."

"Where have I heard that tone before?"

Yeah, rhetorical, and every time I'd heard it before, I was lost to Krissy's allure. Still, there are plenty of worse fates.

I loved the spa bath in the secluded courtyard of my townhouse. The bubbling warm water was relaxing, just as touted in the brochure from Guido's Hot Tub Emporium. But Krissy took relaxation to a divine level. If Guido could put Krissy in their marketing material, they'd sell a shit load more spas. And then probably get charged for corrupting public morals.

Luckily for me, my morals may as well have been inscribed on the dark side of the moon. It wasn't that I was incorruptible: I was so far beyond the possibility of moral corruption as to render the discussion academic.

I was taking a swig of Johnny Walker from the bottle when Krissy did her special tongue thing and I blew my load. Note to self: don't swallow a mouthful of hard liquor at the exact same moment as climaxing. The body can't deal with the competing sensory overloads. I survived, anyway.

Krissy surfaced and gasped for air, but she was grinning as always. What a great girl. With her breath-holding ability, she should have been a tropical pearl diver. Well, in a manner of speaking she was. She did the tongue on teeth move again and I could see she still had a mouthful of gism. She blew me a kiss and did an exaggerated swallow. As I said, what a girl. My own little mermaid, and a lot sexier than that boring bronze one on the rock in Copenhagen.

"My turn, hunky beast."

"Of course, baby."

I grabbed an urgent slug of booze, getting it in microseconds before Krissy's pussy descended on my face. Whiskey with pussy chaser! If you haven't tried it, you haven't lived. Assuming you drink whiskey, that is.

Krissy rode my face until her scream of pleasure defeated any purpose of seclusion. She slid back down into the water and onto my lap.

"Thanks, gorgeous, I needed that."

I kissed her. "So did I."

I passed her the bottle. She took a swig and handed it to me. Then she lit two cigarettes and gave me one.

"Hmm, the house special. You are fantastic, Krissy."

"Ooh, you still do it for me, gorgeous."

My mobile phone, perched on a towel behind the Red Label bottle, started chirping incessantly. It stopped, then immediately restarted.

I leaned back and grabbed it.

I tapped the screen. "Hello?"

A female was crying. "You said you were coming to help me, Mr Clay."

"And I am. Sit tight, I'll be there soon. I had an urgent meeting."

I put the phone down.

Krissy kissed me, grinding her arse on my lap under the water.

"So, handsome, I'm a 'meeting' am I? Well, when I am I going to see you for another meeting?"

I put on a serious face. "When you clean up your act."

She looked equally serious, before cracking up with laughter.

"You couldn't handle clean."

She had me, of course.

"Krissy, baby, the filthier the better. See you soon."

We kissed and I hauled myself out of the spa and away from the temptress that was Krissy.

CHAPTER 3

Thank goodness for the lingering smell of Krissy's wet and wanton crotch in my nostrils, almost as true-blue Aussie as the smell of gum trees. If it hadn't been for the tangy scent and the associated memories, the long drive in the dark out towards Elmore would have been bloody depressing. Melbourne weather in the summer has a meteorologically mind-bending ability to go through four seasons in one day. Since my extra-hot spa bath, the temperature had dropped ten degrees and the rain was coming in sideways with more ferocity than a fishwife's spittle.

The grim weather was fitting for my journey. As the FM radio station started to turn to intermittent static with the increasing distance from the city, my mind turned to my destination. I hadn't been out to Elmore for years. It was one of those small, decaying country towns that should have been called Bleaksville or Miseryvale, something that would give the unwary traveller a hint, a chance to save themselves.

Let me sum up Elmore for you, and the editors of *Lonely Planet* can take my words free of charge. People talk about six degrees of separation. Out here, six my sweet arse. More like two. In these places, and Elmore is just one example, believe me, the definition of a virgin is a twelve-year-old who can outrun her, or his, brothers. And cousins. And uncles. If you close your eyes, you can suck in the predatory twang of the banjos slithering down the breeze from the hills. You open your eyes and realize there are no hills. But the music hasn't stopped. Run, boy, run. The standard greeting in the street is, "G'day, cuz," accompanied by a six-fingered wave. Yeah, they don't need to look at your car rego plates to know you're from out of town. I was damned glad to have Betty the Beretta for company.

The address I was looking for was on the very outskirts of the town. I parked on the wide verge at the front. It was a small cottage in that old Australian style, with red-brick walls and a corrugated-iron roof. Even in the half light of a streetlamp I could see the roof had more rust than paint on it. I looked around before I stepped onto the short front path, running my right hand over my hip to get the reassuring feel of Betty nestled on my belt. The former front lawn looked like a set from *Lawrence of Arabia*. No doubt the result of water restrictions, or a resident who didn't give a rat's, or both. The two survivors in the desert landscape were a large frangipani with white flowers adorning it to the left of the path and a huge oleander shrub to the right. There's a reason those two used to be so ubiquitous in Aussie yards, before all this fancy gardening shit took over. Because they are bloody tough. Tougher than a cockroach in a gas mask with a machine gun.

There was a glow from behind a thin curtain over the window to the right of the front door, and I saw the edge of it twitch. I went up the three steps onto the porch and knocked on the wooden door with its peeling paint and original leadlight insert. The stained glass depicted a pink rose.

"Who is it?"

Still some treacle there, and sounding warm, too. She knew damned well who it was.

"The private investigator you called for, Courtney."

The door opened and a stunning brunette, dressed for display, looked up at me. She had lips so hot they'd be able to defrost an igloo, a body fit to take centre stage in the Louvre, and long, curly, chestnut hair in the eighties style. Think Victoria Principal or Jaclyn Smith, that hot, but just double the cup size. Mind you, there was some rough diamond to her, as well. The eyes told that story. Okay, perhaps the drive to Elmore could turn out not so bleak after all.

"Mister Clay?"

"The one and only, Courtney, and at your service."

"Come in. Thank you so much for coming. Really, thank you."

I stepped into the front hallway. She glanced outside before closing the door and sliding on the security chain.

I followed her into the small front lounge room, admiring the sway of her tight little bum in completely indecent denim shorts. Think Daisy Duke leaning over the hood of the General Lee.

Courtney sat down in a ratty old armchair next to a coffee table covered in women's magazines and two well-fed ashtrays. A bottle of bourbon fought for some real estate with a glass next to it, a splash of brown liquid in the bottom. An old television set was on with some soap opera episode blaring.

She motioned me to the couch at right-angles to her chair. I sat down and lit a smoke. Looking at the mess in front of me I clearly didn't need to ask. She followed suit.

"Tea, coffee, something stronger, Mr Clay?"

"Let's talk first and can you turn that noise down, please?" I pointed at the vapid garbage emanating from the screen.

She got up and went over to the set, giving me another audience with her beautiful butt, and pressed the volume control. The din diminished and she sat back down.

"Remote's broken." She picked up her glass.

"Okay, Courtney, what's the go?"

She cleared her throat. "Well, it's difficult." She went silent.

"Listen, lady, I was supposed to be retired as of a couple of hours ago. And from the looks of things here, I reckon you can't afford me."

"Wait! Please." A tear trickled onto her cheek. The moisture in her eyes made them sparkle and even more attractive. That wasn't going to help me be firm with her.

"So, Courtney, you're going to have to convince me this is pretty important, otherwise I'm walking. Home to a hot bath and some whiskey. And after that who knows."

She leant forward towards me, picking up her purse from the arm of the chair. She pulled a photo out of it and handed it to me.

"This is my son."

It was a young boy, about five or so, not that I'm an expert with kids' ages. Handsome little bugger with strong facial features and a shock of wavy blonde hair. I liked his grin. He'd do damned well with the girlies later.

"Nice looking kid."

More tears started the cascade down her lovely face.

"My baby boy. They've taken him."

I didn't know, yet, what sort of world Courtney lived in, although my mind was making some rapid educated guesses. In any event, this didn't sound good. I looked at her with my sternest look, the one that announced in neon lights that I didn't stand for bullshit.

"Go on. And I want it straight, sweetheart, no crap, understand?"

She nodded as her lips trembled. "This is why I need you, Mister Clay. You're the only one I know who can help me. They've kidnapped my little Archie."

"Hang on. Kidnapped? You should definitely be talking to the police."

"Nope. That's not going to happen, not around here."

"Why not?"

"I've already tried dealing with the cops in this town. It's more delicate than that."

"Obviously."

"And dangerous, Mister Clay."

"Really?" That appealed to my excitable streak. The same one that always landed me up to my eyeballs in strife, and not to mention often up to my nuts in guts. I handed her the photo and she put it on the table.

"Listen, Courtney, I usually catch cheating boyfriends, people who owe money, that sort of thing. But missing persons, especially kidnapped ones, I don't know."

She got up and went over to a cabinet, returning with a second glass. She sat on the edge of her chair, her knee resting against mine. She put her hand on my thigh. Oh, man! That felt like a practiced hand and it was oozing intent. She looked right into my eyes. Syrup returned by the bucketful.

"Jasper, can I offer you a drink?"

Her smouldering brown eyes told me that something came with the drink. And it wasn't ice cubes or a swizzle stick.

Two sips into my bourbon, another ciggie on the go, and Courtney decided the armchair was no longer comfortable, but apparently my lap was. She straddled me, her taut cleavage nestling under my chin. She probably detected the movement in my pants and she gently ground my crotch with hers. That had the erection complete in a microsecond. Her hand wasn't the only practiced part of her anatomy, that was for certain. I rapidly concluded this assignment was going be another one with payment in kind, my services for hers.

Long foreplay sessions on the couch are for teenagers and religious types. I'm neither. I swallowed my drink, stubbed out my ciggie, and squeezed Courtney's butt cheeks hard with both my hands. She sighed and ground more firmly.

I picked her up as she stuck her tongue down my throat.

She clung onto me, her thighs wrapped around my waist, all the way the bedroom. I threw her onto the bed and she growled at me, those brown eyes now on fire. I threw my jacket on the ground as she pulled me onto the bed and started ripping at my clothes. I unclipped my Beretta and Courtney took hold of it, running her finger over its handle and along the length of the holster. There was something wildly erotic about that. She put the gun into the drawer of the bedside table and undid my belt. My partner in crime burst out of my boxer shorts, as hard as a rock. She wrapped her fingers around my shaft as I ripped her blouse off and extricated her from those shorts. Her body, in her crimson lace underwear, so skimpy that skimpy itself would have felt short-changed, was smoking hot, off the scale, in fact.

I groaned as she took my cock into her mouth and pushed me onto my back. She sucked for a minute and then lifted her head to smile at me. She slid up my body as her eyes burned with hungry intent, like a carpet python slithering into the henhouse. As she sat astride me, I noticed the knickers were crotchless, not that they needed any less fabric to them to start with. But then I felt the warmth of her wet pussy envelop my cock and I wanted to sing the praises of crotchless underwear.

The ride was slow and expert, her face coming down to kiss me and my hands inside the equally flimsy bra, massaging her superb breasts. She then sat back up, riding slowly still, and started fingering her clitoris. Her rubbing became more frenzied and her riding increased its tempo. It was heaven, or at least the equivalent for a heathen like me. Just as my loins boiled over and exploded inside her, I felt the clamping of her orgasm and her shriek just about ruptured my ear drums. I hadn't experienced timing that exquisite in a long while. Like I said, expert. I had no doubt now what Courtney did for a living.

She flopped down beside me.

"Like that, sugar?"

"Fucking fantastic, thank you."

"So, are you hired?"

"Was that the retainer?"

She smiled. "Call it what you like. There's plenty more of that available."

She sat up and grabbed her cigarettes from the bedside table. She lit two and passed one to me.

"Listen, Jasper, there is something I really have to tell you."

"Hush. We can talk the assignment later. I think there are much better things to be doing right now." I ran my fingers into her wet crotch.

She groaned. "But, Jasper, my son is..."

Her sentence was cut off by the crash of breaking glass and splintering timber.

She screamed and stood up to look out the bedroom door.

"Get back here, Courtney!" I rolled to go for my Beretta. As I did so I got tangled in sheets and clothing. It wasn't a very graceful manoeuvre by a knight in shining armour going to the rescue of his damsel, that was for sure. As I fell off the bed, taking the bedside table over, it was far more like a Monty Python sketch. Scrabbling for the drawer, wishing she'd left the gun on the top, I turned to see two nasty-looking shitheads, one slim, one fat, and both in black leather jackets. The fat one slapped Courtney hard, knocking her over. The other goon pulled out a black rubber cosh that had my name written all over it. I could almost make out the letters of my name as it descended at speed onto my head, with the goon showing off his linguistic range and ability. "Take this, cunt!"

The room was spinning and my vision was littered with stars. I saw the fat goon throw Courtney over his shoulder.

He looked at me, laughed, and said, "That blow's gonna give him brain damage, I reckon."

My new friend just grunted.

Things started to go dark.

It was lights out for Jasper Clay.

CHAPTER 4

Fuck, I was in pain!

As I came to on the floor, I reached for my throbbing head, and not in the good sense. I felt some moisture and crustiness. I pulled my hand back to my face, smelling the metallic blood scent and then seeing the reddish-brown smear on my fingers.

I pulled my knees up under my gut and rolled onto them. From there I got unsteadily to my feet. I stumbled and fell onto the bed, which looked like a warzone. My face landed in a wet spot. Aside from my own juice, I could smell pussy. I managed a half smile through the pain.

It was coming back to me.

I scrabbled over the mattress to the overturned bedside table and pulled open the drawer that was ajar. My Beretta was still lying in there. I grabbed Betty and took some comfort from the feel of the customized grip.

The drawer fell out as I retrieved my gat. A large, rolled wad of cash fell on the floor. I picked it up, of course. Shit, they were hundreds. Must have been at least five grand in there. After I clipped Betty on my belt, I shoved the wad in my trouser pocket. Yeah, this dame could afford me, it turned out.

Well, the absent dame, that is.

I walked into the hallway and saw the front door was closed, although the timber frame around the lock and chain was fractured. Then I went to the bathroom. I wasn't normally a fan of myself in the mirror, but this morning was particularly ugly. The gash on my crown was on the verge of needing stitches, but given Courtney was missing stroke abducted, and her kid was missing stroke abducted, sitting around in Emergency for three hours plus waiting for our health system was not on my cards.

I rummaged in the vanity drawer and found some Dettol and bandages. Sort of stuff you'd expect a mum with a young kid to have: lots of scrapes to tend to.

Fuckity, fuck, fuck, fuck!!! The Dettol stung more than the fucking clap. And I should know.

First aid rendered, I washed my hands and stared at the mirror.

"Morning, Jasper," I said. "So, did you get lucky last night? Well, did ya, punk?"

I do love the Dirty Harry lines. I thought of the pussy scent again, and I smiled.

"Yes, Jasper my old son, don't know about lucky given the beating, but she wasn't a bad score at all."

Yep, Courtney had been hot and genuine. And I like that in a woman. Something still tickled my recesses. Never mind, time for bloody coffee.

I found the kitchen and some Nescafé instant. Any port in a storm. And it could have been worse: it could have been International Roast. I boiled the kettle, dumped two heaped spoons of coffee into a mug along with an equal amount of sugar. I opened the fridge, pulled out a milk carton and took a sniff. Old habits. Yep, that was okay.

I carried my mug of revival through to the lounge room. I sat down on the couch, the one that had led to my capitulation last night. The photo of her missing kid was lying on the table. I picked it up and stared at it as I sipped my coffee. He was a good-looking kid, that was undeniable.

"Where are you, little one? Where the hell are you? And who are these people around here?"

My mind returned to my chat with Courtney last night, before it all got steamy and horizontal.

I pulled out my notebook that I'd been jotting stuff in as we had been chatting.

Courtney had sure sounded fair dinkum when she said, "My little boy means so much to me, Jasper." She was sobbing. "And that arsehole Danvers took him away from me."

"Who's Danvers?" I'd asked.

"He's a creep, a thug, and he runs this damned town. He owns most of it, and a lot of us. I work for him, Jasper."

She'd paused, then resumed in a husky whisper. "Jasper, I'm a working girl."

She might have thought that would be shameful in many men's eyes, but not lecherous Jasper Clay. The tally of prostitutes I'd enjoyed over the years was higher than the entire Vatican hierarchy's scoreboard of altar boys.

And as I'd looked at sexy, sultry Courtney, definitely way too classy a working girl for this shithole of a town, I had gone into autopilot to add to my tally. Damn, she'd been a hell of a great root. Those bastards had cut short what was destined to be a night of debauchery to occupy its own chapter in the Jasper Clay memoirs. And, of course, they'd abducted Courtney.

I looked at my notes: "Working girl, Elmore, Danvers, child, kidnap. Motive?"

Yep, I had been pondering that last query when Courtney dropped the acid on me last night.

So, motive? Well, maybe this working girl had not been playing by Danvers's rules, or maybe she'd spoken to the wrong person about wanting to get out. Lots of maybes.

I looked at the photo of the little lad again. "Talk to me, son."

My car keys were on the table where I'd left them. I swallowed my coffee and psyched my sore head to swing into action.

It was pissing down again as I drove out of Elmore. I needed to see a contact of mine and I was guessing she'd be somewhere around Melbourne on the job. The job with a badge, that is.

As I drove down the main drag there was a collection of the local guys gathered under the awnings at the front of the small shopping centre. Mullets and flannel shirts were clearly the height of fashion for the local knuckle-draggers, the bogans of Elmore. Yep, this was bogan central. Our Aussie bogan towns were up there with the best of the American redneck versions.

Now, you know that pictogram called The March of Progress? Yeah, the one with a monkey, then an ape, then *Homo neanderthalensis*, then *Homo sapiens*. When you get to experience real bogans, you realize that the picture is missing a step: *Homo boganis*. And he slots in before the Neanderthal, just after the chimp.

I cleared the ugly, inbred town and stopped at a service station on the highway. I fuelled up and then got on the phone. I smiled as I pressed the contact name. Yeh, you guessed it, some more delectable carnal memories.

"Coffy, it's Jasper."

"Ooh, my favourite PI. And to what do I owe the pleasure of this call? Jasper want some action or Jasper want some information?"

I laughed. "Oh, Coffy, you know me too well."

"Actually, Jasper, I know you obscenely well. Action or info, babe?"

"I'd settle for both, Coffy."

It was her turn to laugh. "Cool. You tell me what info you need and then you come meet me, and we'll settle the action. I'm on a job, so it's hush hush about who I am."

"Understood, detective."

"So, shoot." She cackled at her own pun.

"Coffy, you're a darling and a great detective, but please don't ever go into comedy."

She cackled again.

"So, my target is a bloke called Danvers out in Elmore. Apparently runs the town and controls the girl trade. So, I'm guessing he controls the drugs, too. Need whatever you can get. And I'll make it up to you."

"Jasper, you have no idea what I'll extract from you this time. Give me two hours. Ready for the location?"

"Yep." I jotted it down in my notebook. "I can make that in two, so all good. See you soon, sweetheart."

She blew me a kiss and hung up.

Just over two hours later, I pulled up outside the address. It was a community centre in Werribee, distinctly shabby, which suited the area, and currently closed. Normally I'd be suspicious, but I knew and trusted Coffy. Well, when a lady, and not literally you understand, has let you do all that stuff with her, then she's earned some trust.

My phone buzzed with a message.

COME AROUND TO THE BACK DOOR.

I smiled and texted back.

NOT THE FIRST TIME YOU'VE SAID THAT.

I got out of the car and stepped straight in a puddle the depth of the Mariana Trench.

I locked the chariot and trudged around the back of the building.

The back door opened as I approached it and Coffy's grinning face greeted me. She wasn't classically beautiful, but she was pretty in the face and she had a good body that she kept in fine shape at the gym. Oh, and a complete absence of morals. Always an essential quality in a woman, in my view.

She closed the door and wrapped her arms around my neck, locked her lips onto mine, and launched her tongue into my mouth like a torpedo. That was "hello" in Coffy-speak.

I had to disengage first as I needed oxygen.

"And good to see you, too, Coffy."

"Been a while between visits, Jasper. Your business been quiet?"

"Yeah, plus I'm packing it in. This is my last gig."

She pouted. "So my Jasper won't be wanting info again?"

"No, but I'll always take your action."

"Oh. That's all right then. Come on through."

She led me into a pool room.

"So, Coffy, what the hell is the covert unit doing with this?"

21

"Intel is that it's become the centre of the local amphet trade, so I am the new 'manager' come in to run the centre for a few months, and gather all the drum we can."

"I see."

"So, Jasper, I'm sticking my neck out this time, honey. Could blow my cover getting a visit from an out-of-town bloke."

"Sorry, sweetheart, but I really do need this info on Danvers."

She picked up an envelope off a cabinet and handed it to me as I leant against the pool table. "Everything I can get without raising any flags on the system. I just logged my searches as being connected with the drug trade here. And Danvers is up to his neck in drugs and tarts."

"You're a gem, Coffy."

"I know. Now what am I going to get?"

I grinned at her. "What do you want?"

"Well, you kinda owe me big for last time, remember?"

I was confused, but not for long. My synapses fired and that brief encounter in the car came back to me. It had literally been a five-minute meeting, but the head job Coffy gave me qualified for its own sequel in the *Fast and Furious* franchise. Then she'd had to run.

All the girls want to give me head. All the guys want to belt me in the head. Guess that makes me a ladies' man rather than a man's man. I'm cool with that.

She raised her eyebrows. "Remember, Jasper?"

"Yep. My turn to head south."

"For starters, and then plenty more."

She pushed me backwards onto the pool table and undid my belt and trousers. I wasn't clothed for long, and nor was she. She shuffled along the green baize on her knees until her pussy, moist and pungent already, hovered above my face.

She looked down at me. "And there's no dessert until you've eaten all your meat."

There was no chance to respond before I was smothered in the valley of lost souls.

CHAPTER 5

It was mid-afternoon and I had driven back north. I'd stopped in a lay-by just before the intersection with the sign announcing turn right for Elmore. The sign had three bullet holes in it. I'd stopped to take some Nurofen for my pounding headache. I checked over my case scribblings in my notebook, thinking about my next move. I set my phone alarm for two hours hence, locked the doors, and dozed off.

There was a knocking in my head, but at least the throbbing had subsided. No, the beat wasn't in my head, some dude was tapping on the window staring in at me. Fuck, couldn't a man get rest anywhere?

"Hey, bro," the face yelled.

It had started raining again so I simply yelled back through the glass, feeling for the comfort of my Beretta. "What do you want?"

"Wind your window down, bro."

I did a touch, but not enough for him to get a hand through, in case that was his game. "First, I am not your fucking bro. Second, and to repeat myself, what the fuck do you want?"

"I was just trying to hitch a lift into town, and now it's raining."

"You want a ride, is that it?"

"Yes, please, bro...sorry. That would be awesome."

"Well, buddy, I'm going roughly in that direction. Hop in."

He scooted around to the passenger side as I unlocked the doors and cleared the map book (yeah, shoot me, I'm old school) and drink bottle off the passenger seat.

He plonked himself down and put his seat belt on.

"Hey, thanks, man. I saw you were asleep and wasn't sure whether to wake you up. But I was a bit sick of walking and it started to rain."

"Where exactly you headed?"

I spotted a tattoo on the inside of his left forearm. It looked like a kickboxer in action with the inscription "Club D".

He caught me looking at it and hastily pulled down his sleeve. "Head into town and I'll direct you from there."

I nodded at him, started the engine and put the radio on. I got onto the road and swung right towards Elmore.

"So, where is this place you're going?"

"Up ahead, not far. You been here before?"

"Don't think so, buddy."

I reached for a stick of gum. He spotted the packet in the dash console and looked at me.

"You want one?"

He grinned. "Yeah, man, can I?"

"Help yourself."

"Awesome, thanks,"

He stuck a piece of gum in his pie hole and then his foot went up on the dashboard.

"Don't get too comfy, buddy, this isn't your car. And there's always more walking."

"Oh, sorry, man."

His foot dropped back to the floor.

"My name's Brodie, by the way."

I nodded and grunted at him. I wasn't giving anything in return. This bogan certainly didn't need my name.

We drove on in silence for a couple of minutes, now into the built-up area.

"Here it is, man, this is my stop." He indicated a warehouse building on the left.

I pulled up out the front. The rain had stopped.

As he opened the door to get out, I could hear some raucous yelling from the building, like a crowd noise.

As he walked towards the shed, he pumped his fist at me and grinned.

My interest was piqued. And I wasn't alone on that regard. I'd noticed what had to be a cop surveillance car as we'd pulled up to the joint. That bloke was sticking out more than a Rottweiler lying on its back with a big lipstick erection. Still, no harm in me having a discreet gander as well.

I parked the wheels and sauntered back to the warehouse, finding a gap in the side wall big enough to look through.

It was noisy inside all right, and a fair crowd. It was a fight club with a sparring platform in the middle, roped in like a normal boxing ring. But instead of two muscly, ugly blokes punching each other, this was a bit more entertaining.

Two fit girlies, both very early twenties, were going at each other with fists and feet. They both wore tight, really tight, shorts, and crop tops. One was in blue and one in red. And aside from great toned and lithe bodies, they were both pretty in the face, too. I wouldn't have said no to wrestling with those two, but preferably in Jello and butt-naked.

Judging by the yelling from the crowd around the ropes, the girl in blue was called Mel and Sara was the one in red. Sara certainly had most of the crowd with her.

They were both landing a few blows, punches and kicks, but then Sara got a vicious-looking heel kick into Mel's guts and she went down onto the canvas.

"Take that, bitch!" she yelled, standing over her fallen opponent.

The crowd went berserk and I saw Brodie supplicating to a large man sitting on a chair, clad in a long leather coat and wearing those dark wrap-around sunnies, like Louie the Fly. Sunglasses of the true bogan class, if you ask me. All thug-chic fashion with no class.

The seated guy, the only seated person in the place, oozed the "I'm the fucking boss" aura, and Brodie's fawning, as well as the two goons, one fat and one slim, standing in an almost regimental manner behind him, gave the overwhelming impression of bogan royalty. I wondered if that was Danvers, the man who ran the town. Could match the "Club D" inscribed on the back wall.

Personally, when it comes to royalty, I've always been a fan of the French solution: off with their heads. But that seems to upset all the sentimental types these days, not to mention the woke wankers.

The big man was nodding approvingly at Sara, the fighter in red. The crowd shouting was giving her their love as well.

The blue girl, Mel, hauled herself up off the mat and charged at Sara. There was some wrestling and grappling to start with, which I found rather erotic to be honest, before Sara succeeded in shoving Mel backwards and then punching her smack in the face. As Mel reeled backwards from that, Sara went in with two swift kicks to the abdomen and then an old-fashioned haymaker that just about snapped Mel's head off her neck. That would have been a crying shame. Pretty head, pretty neck, sensational bod.

As it was, Mel was down for the count. Part of me wanted to crash my way in there and give lovely Mel the kiss of life. But I wouldn't have wanted to deal with Miss Sara's feet and hands, that's a definite. Ouch, that would hurt, big time.

I dragged my lascivious gaze away from the fighting girls and focussed in on the big man and his entourage. There were wads of cash flowing around like bodily fluids at a brothel. Clearly quite a few punters had won on Sara's victory.

I saw Brodie go up to Sara, give her a drink bottle, and help her down from the ring. Mel still lay on the canvas.

Okay, time for snooping Jasper to go. I'd seen all I was going to, and I had an assignment to get back to.

Although, my ever suspicious and cynical mind told me that there was an overlap here.

That big man in there was someone, and in this lowbrow incestual town there was probably only one someone: Danvers. Plus, those two thugs could easily have been the Laurel and Hardy duo from last night.

I sauntered back to my car. The dog-penis surveillance cop was still sitting on the street. He may as well have had a fucking blue flashing light. What a clown.

I hopped in my wheels and discreetly sidled off, pulling up around the block to look at my notes and the map, and decide my next move.

As I sat there, a metallic-blue BMW Roadster cruised up next to me and came to a halt. The big man from the fight club was driving and alone. The shaved dog-ugly head with the black wrap-around sunnies was instantly recognisable. A muscly forearm rested on the sill, a tattoo showing, "Club D".

He eye-balled me and then planted his foot on the gas. There was a squeal of rubber and he was gone.

Big man, big ego, small cock. Always the way, I reckoned.

CHAPTER 6

I was shattered and needed some uninterrupted shuteye: no wanton wenches and no nasty bastards.

As I sidled down the main road into town, I came across the ubiquitous country-town motel, with its pot-holed driveway and gaudy flashing sign with a couple of the neon tubes blown. Out the front, a couple of once graceful palm trees were clinging to life like refugees. That sort of summed up my own feelings, so I pulled into the near-empty car park. There were two tradesman's vans and a rusty people mover. Guessed I wasn't likely to be pulling any action in this joint. No loss at this point as I just needed to sleep the sleep of the righteous. Not that anyone has ever used that word to describe me, but they can all bugger off.

I parked the car and sauntered into the shabby reception foyer at the front. One of those old-fashioned doorbells jangled as I went in. What emerged from the back room was anything but shabby. Despite my fatigue, I got some distinct movement. Credit to her. Rolling brown hair, high cheekbones, lips that were made for action, and a barely covered rack ruining the elastic in a boob-tube. Classy establishment, really. And my sort of joint, no risk.

She gazed at me. Now that was a come-fuck-me smile if ever I saw one.

"Hello, handsome." Her lioness eyes drilled into me as if I was her next meal out on the Serengeti.

"I really need a bed. Been on the road too long, and some other shit. How much for a room?"

I didn't actually care, but it seemed the standard question at this juncture. I grabbed a wad of cash from my back pocket.

"That'll be eighty, sugar. And check out is at ten." She leaned towards me.

"Done." I counted out eighty in redbacks and put it on the counter.

Her fingers brushed my hand as she scooped up the notes. But her eyes never left my face.

Still looking at me—damn, I'd hate to play this chick at poker—she reached behind her and grabbed a key. "Now, sugar, you need anything at all, you call me. And sleep well, if that's what you want."

Bloody hell, talk about having it served on a plate. But seriously, I did need to sleep.

"Thanks, babe. I'll bear that in mind."

I took my key as she stared at me, the tip of her tongue just visible as it massaged her top front teeth.

No, Jasper, it's bedtime, brother. I reluctantly trudged off and up the outside stairs to the first floor where my room was situated.

In I went. I could feel her watching me. I could feel my loins. I had to sleep, fuck it. I closed the door behind me. The shabby exterior of the motel was reflected in the dated interior of the room. But at least it seemed clean. I went to the dunny and then peeled off my gear and slid into the overly firm bed. And that was that, lights out.

As I came to, I half registered a body in the room and then there was light, with the curtains moving back from the window. I could smell coffee, and perfume. At this time in the morning, a tough choice which was more alluring. My eyes focussed and I realised the source of the perfume scent. The girl from the reception desk was standing there, clad in two fifths of fuck all. Well, my imagination didn't need to turn up for class this morning. She was grinning at me, that tongue moving over teeth again.

I turned to the coffee smell and saw a tray on the bedside table: coffee, juice and toast with eggs.

I looked back at the apparition that would have given the Pope a morning glory. "Oh, breakfast?"

"I got you scrambled eggs, juice, toast. And coffee, of course. Figured you'd need some energy after that big sleep, handsome."

"Cool, thanks, that's great."

I took a swig of juice and then started on the coffee. It was good.

"I didn't know breakfast was included, though."

She laughed. "Yes, yes it is. Well, sort of." That smile and that tongue.

I was barring up. "What do you mean by 'sort of?'"

She ran her fingers over one breast, down to her crotch, and then back up to her mouth where she licked them. Fuck, now I was fully barred up.

"Well, I'm not supposed to, but you seem like a real nice guy."

"You're not supposed to? But this is a motel, right, so there must be a food menu?"

She glanced at the window.

"Well, yes it is. But Ralph doesn't like me taking room service to the men guests. He usually does that and I tend to the lady guests."

I chewed on some toast with some egg. It was good. Another swill of coffee.

"Babe, in this day and age, when you're running an establishment like this, I reckon having to separate genders is bloody ridiculous."

She grinned. "You're funny, and handsome. I like you."

My erection and I had a lot more than "like" in mind.

"So, is Ralph your boyfriend? And the owner?"

"No! I'm the owner. My daddy left it to me. It's a job and I kinda like it. But Ralph..."

"Kinda like it?"

"I like having my business, but men in this town. It's complicated."

I pointed to the breakfast tray, indicating she could have some. She took a sip of juice.

"Thanks."

"So, it's 'complicated'?"

"We don't get nice looking guys like you around here often."

I chuckled. "You mean bruised, battered and broken-hearted men?"

She giggled and put her hand on the top of my thigh which was under the sheet.

"Oh, stop it. You look bloody fine to me, handsome. And I'm sure I can help with a broken heart."

I chewed some more toast and egg. "Thanks, babe."

She glanced at my boner and her hand slid up my thigh. "In fact, I haven't had a good root in a long time. A very long time."

"Is that so? There's obviously something wrong with the blokes in this town then." Well, I knew the answer to that already.

In a flash she was on top of me and had removed her dress. She leant down and stuck her tongue down my throat. The girl could kiss. I reckoned that wasn't all she'd be good at.

She came up for air. "I'm Cuddles." She undid her bra, letting a delicious pair loose in the steamy air above me.

"I like that name, Cuddles."

She smiled and smothered my face with her breasts.

It's bloody hard yakka this PI gig, I tell you.

Next thing I know, it's just got even harder, and I'm not talking about my rod. If that got any harder it'd split open like an over-stuffed banana.

Cuddles was now on all fours and had lost her knickers, or the scrap of lace that had been posing for the part. She was true blue Aussie, but down there was straight out of Rio. And Rio on a rainy day.

"I love doggy-style, handsome." With that I got an eyeful of her rear end, proffered to me like a nymphomaniac baboon.

Duty stations, Jasper! And I was out from under the sheet quicker than a politician telling a lie. Cuddles groaned as I slid in and told me to hurry up and nail her.

That I did and had just blown my load when Cuddles suddenly leapt off the bed and grabbed for her underwear.

"Fuck, fuck, fuck!"

I was confused. It's not like I'd done anything she didn't want or wasn't expecting, like a surprise back door visit.

"What is it?"

"It's Ralph! He's back sooner than he said."

"You're kidding me." Last complication I needed was facing a pissed-off boyfriend whose girl I'd just banged.

"No, it's him. He's looking around for me at reception." She slid her dress back on.

"What do you want me to do, Cuddles?" I was getting my gear on pronto, too. Fronting the cuckolded bloke would be bad enough, but I never liked the idea of a showdown whilst butt naked.

She didn't answer, just stared out the window.

"Cuddles? What do I do?"

"Um, I don't know. Just stay here. I'll pretend I'm doing the housekeeping, clearing the plates, you know."

"Hang on."

"What?"

"You said you weren't supposed to bring me breakfast, remember?"

"Shit, he's coming."

She picked up the tray and opened the room door. Just as she went to step out, this fat, greasy meathead in dirty jeans and black leather jacket bounded up the concrete stairs and stopped outside on the walkway, fronting Cuddles. He was one from the fight club.

He looked in at me. Talk about stink-eye. And now I was also sure he was the fat goon who carried Courtney out of her house last night.

He turned back to Cuddles and stuck his finger in her face, then pointed it in my direction. "So, you made him breakfast, did you?"

"Yes, hun."

Why do gorgeous girls gravitate to total deadshit arseholes? It really is one of the great unanswered questions in life, I reckon.

Ralph glared at me. Maybe he could pick up the post-coital glow that must have been covering my smug mug. Or maybe the miasma of wet, urgent sex was wafting out from the room.

He grabbed her by her jaw. "And I suppose I'm expected to believe that's all you gave him, huh?!"

Cuddles wrenched her jaw free. "I'm just trying to do my job, baby."

She started sobbing, although it was obviously forced.

Ralph, classy gentleman that he was, glared at Cuddles and shoved his hand up her short dress. He withdrew and stuck his fingers under his nose.

"So, is a wet pussy a side order on the breakfast menu now?"

I thought about chipping in a juicy one-liner about kippers, but just smiled to myself. Had to be ready for wherever this was going.

Cuddles tried to move away from Ralph, but he grabbed her wrist.

"I can smell the sex on you, girl!"

Cuddles started crying for real this time.

Ralph didn't come across as the progressive type in terms of women's rights, rather I pegged him as the possessive, controlling type. Middle initials of A.V.O. I figured this was going downhill.

As if he was reading my mind, Ralph gave Cuddles a backhander across her face, knocking her onto the concrete floor of the walkway balcony. Yeah, he wasn't a mind-reader, just another toxic male wanker. Okay, Jasper, action stations, son.

As I stepped through the doorway, Ralph turned and shaped up, another rush of testosterone motivating him. He was only about three centimetres taller than me, but he had about thirty kilos extra weight and there was muscle, as well as fat. The malevolent glint in his eyes told me he was looking forward to hurting me.

Enter Betty stage left.

I whipped the Beretta from my belt and stuck it under his chin as he reached me. He wasn't remotely ready for that move, and the glare of malice instantly morphed into a nervous anxiety.

Cuddles was hauling herself back to her feet, wide eyes looking at my gat.

I sneered at Ralph, getting close to his ugly face, which resembled a Mediterranean bulldog that had been hit in the mouth with a baseball bat. Again, what the fuck did Cuddles see in this piece of shit?

I grinned now. "Real tough wanker, aren't you, belting women." I pushed the gun barrel into his flesh. "Do not ever hit her again, especially in the face, arsehole."

He stared at me and I was pretty sure I could detect the rancid tang of fresh urine.

"If I ever hear you have, I'm coming back, fuckstain. Got it?"

"Okay, okay! Got it. It won't happen again."

"Now, apologize to the lady."

"I'm sorry," gasped Ralph, still staring at me.

"Apologize to her, dipshit, not me."

I slid the Beretta up his face as he turned towards Cuddles.

"I'm sorry, baby."

"Really?"

"Yes, really."

"How sorry, Ralph?"

"Jesus, baby, I'm not worthy of you."

I couldn't stay silent on this point. "Damned right there, fuckstain. Don't know why she's with you."

"Go on, Ralphy," said Cuddles.

"Baby, I'll make it up to you."

"And what do you have in mind?"

"Baby, those sheepskin slippers you wanted."

For fuck's sake was all I could think. Why couldn't women drag themselves away from these arseholes? Same old story. Okay, I'd done all I could. I stepped back from

Ralph as he moved towards Cuddles. Now she had her hand on his face.

"Oh, Ralphy. Get me those hot pink ones like you goddamn said you would."

"Okay, baby, anything for you."

I tried to hold down the vomit as I walked down the stairs. Neither of them were paying me the slightest bit of attention now.

As I opened my car door, I was still within earshot of the couple.

"You promise me?" said Cuddles.

"Of course, baby, I love you," oozed Ralph.

Fuck me, it was like a scene of *Romeo and Juliet* rewritten by the Iranian Ministry of Truth.

I drove out onto the highway.

CHAPTER 7

I needed some relax and thinking time, and without any exchange of love juices. I spotted an empty car park beside some closed industrial workshops, so I pulled in there and cut the motor. Nice and out of harm's way. Yeah righto, Jasper, as if.

I'd only been there for about a quarter of an hour, enjoying the crisp, fresh air and going over my notes and pondering plans, when I heard a couple of motorbike engines. And they were ones with a bit of grunt, not some 125cc pretenders. I saw them in my rear-vision mirror coming into the car park. They were a couple of Kawasaki 750s with two riders all in coloured leather, one red and one yellow, with full-face visor helmets. Okay, so it wasn't the local Comancheros or Hells Angels then. Probably just a couple of biker lads out oozing testosterone with the big throbbing machines between their legs. Wankers.

The red one pulled alongside my car and stopped next to my open window.

I looked at the smoked-glass visor, saw nothing.

"Mate, I'm busy, what do you want?"

His answer was a leather-gloved fist smacking me in the face. Fuck, that hurt.

Next thing I knew was my door was open and both of these dudes were hauling me out of my wheels. I took a wild swing, but just connected with a helmet. Fuck, that hurt, too.

Then it started raining fists. I went down and copped some boots in my guts. I blacked out when one of the boots connected with my head.

I came to with the sound of revving Kawasaki engines. I was lying on my back, still next to my car where I had fallen under the beating. I lifted my head off the concrete to look at the bikers. They revved louder still.

Fuck me! I saw a chain looped around my ankles and trailing off to the yellow rider's bike. He inched forward, taking up the slack in the chain until it was taut. Fuck, this was not how I had envisaged leaving the planet. My two preferred options were going down in a hail of bullets in a noble gunfight with scumbags or having a sudden but entirely blissful coronary whilst chock-a-block up some gorgeous tart's pussy. Not time to go yet, Jasper, and sure as hell not like this.

I felt the chain start to drag and I pulled my Beretta out, took the most careful aim of my entire dissolute life, and let three rounds go. The chain shackling my ankles gave way and I jumped to my feet.

I levelled Betty at the shithead bikers and smiled at them. It was tempting to plug the cunts here and now, but I did not need the coppers involved. I took up a shooting stance and that was enough for the leather heroes.

Two Kawasakis left two trails of rubber as they screamed out of the car park and disappeared.

Well, Jasper, looks like you've kicked the hornet's nest in this bumfuck town. Gloves are off now.

CHAPTER 8

I walked into the Scarlet Tiger. I'd noted it down from my chat with Courtney. I heard the buzzer sound deeper in the premises as I stepped over the threshold. The front reception area, empty of humans, was all subdued lighting, red and purple lace draped over lamps, and some half-pleasant patchouli incense burning in the corner. I smiled to myself. I always love the irony of a brothel's front of house with its delicate scents and pretence at allure. In the rooms out back, any allure is quickly replaced with primal grunting, either determined or desperate, or both. And patchouli is usurped by the pungent tang of wet pussy and the cloying reek of expended gism.

On the counter was the menu, the catalogue of the available flesh. I flicked through. Yep, for a bumfuck town like this, there was certainly some fine dining on offer.

Before I could finish my perusal, the receptionist appeared from the corridor behind the counter.

"G'day, handsome. I'm Cindy and I'm here to help you find what you're looking for." She smiled like a dentist's advert, the nicotine stains notwithstanding. She was bottle blonde, plump, and past it. Once she would have worked out back, but at least ten years ago.

"Well, hello Cindy."

"So quiet today that I was beginning to think that men didn't want sex anymore. Still, bloody inflation, we're all to blame, aren't we?"

She took a gulp from the glass of sparkling wine in her hand.

"Yeah, I'm more into the ladies than economics."

"Or maybe it's the new competition. That bloody Opalite joint up the road has been taking my clientele, I'm sure of it. That fucking Danvers arsehole is to blame."

As she smacked one hand on the countertop, her other hand jerked with its glass and a splash of wine sloshed onto the menu. I glanced down and saw Courtney's face staring saucily at me from the page I hadn't quite fixed my gaze on when Cindy had arrived.

She picked up the menu book and wiped it down with some tissues from under the counter.

"Sorry, handsome, very clumsy of me."

"No problems."

"Now, where were we?"

"I..."

"That's right, sex. Now I'm sure you'll be wanting the very best time tonight."

I nodded. Well, there wasn't a night I could ever think of when the very best sex wasn't the optimal choice. Sadly, it was often not the realistic one. Not that there's any such thing in my book as a bad fuck. Well, as long as you're not in a prison shower block and you're the one being the bitch, that sure classes as bad. But as long as your hard cock is sliding into a wet pussy, it cannot by definition be bad, as such. But then there's a whole scale of sex that's mediocre-good through to sex that transforms your life view, the sex that has you with your eyes clamped shut and your brain screaming, "I want to fucking die right now because it will never be better than this". And when none of anything on the spectrum is on offer, then it's Missus Palmer and her five daughters. Not the worst orgasms I've had, let me tell you.

"So, sweetheart, I've got Debbie and Wendy working tonight. Both lovely girls."

"You mentioned Danvers?"

"Yeah. A right prick and old-school thug. Most of my girls are now working for him. I'm going to have to close down soon."

"I see. Shame."

"Yeah, that's life, too. Listen, sweetheart, you after information or a root?"

"Always on the hunt for both, but info is the priority right now."

She chuckled and chugged down the rest of her wine. "I need a refill. Listen, sweetheart, head down the hallway there to the breakout room. Jake, one of my lads is there, he knows heaps about this town."

"Cool."

She turned to the corridor entrance. "Jakey!" she yelled.

"Yeah, Cind?" was shouted back from the depths of the premises.

"You decent or you with one of the girls?"

"I'm decent. Watching a film."

"Fella here wants to talk, wants info about the town."

"Okay, Cind."

"Head on down there, handsome. Jakey's a darling, and very sexy. I like 'em like that. He's a bit arrogant at first, but just chat with him. And that'll be a hunge up front." She held out her hand.

I peeled two pineapples out of my wallet and placed them in her hand.

The phone rang on the counter and she turned to pick it up. "Good evening, Scarlet Tiger. Home to the best booty and boobs in the region."

I doubted that, but I wasn't here to do a review. I tapped my forehead and headed down the hallway.

I could hear the TV coming from the open doorway at the end.

"G'day, mate," I said to the slimy dude sitting at a table watching the screen.

He turned, looking irritated, a cigarette smouldering as it hung from his lower lip. There was a glass of bourbon on the table, next to the bottle.

He grunted at me.

"I paid Cindy, mate, so now we're going to talk."

"So, what's your deal, man?"

"I'm looking for a friend. A lady."

"In here, man, all the chicks will be your friend, if the price is right."

"So, quiet in here?"

"And?"

"Listen, mate, given I've just paid your boss for this little chat, how about you drop the fucking attitude and start with a bit of good old-fashioned customer service."

"Listen, buddy, I really couldn't give a shit about whatever you've got going on. Say what you want to say and then fuck off."

Fuck me, talk about failing the attitude exam with an F minus. Mind you, I doubted this fucktard would even get his own name right on the top of the paper.

"You didn't listen to what I said about attitude, did you?"

He glared at me and started to stand up.

I pulled back my jacket to show off the Beretta. "Not so fast, pal. This can get very nasty, very quickly. Believe me."

The sneering glare turned to wide-eyed anxiety. "Okay, okay."

"I'm looking for a girl named Courtney."

"Don't know her."

I pointed at the copy of the menu book on the table. "Open it and start turning the pages."

He complied.

"Stop there. That's her."

He shook his head again.

Wrong answer. I drew my gun and pointed it at him. "Fucking try again, Jakey."

"Come on, man, this is bullshit."

"I'm not going to use it, mate. Or am I? Big question for you right this moment, Jakey. Now tell me where she is."

"Man, seriously I don't know. That girl used to be here, but I don't know her real name. They all use pseudonyms."

Fuck me backwards, I wasn't expecting that sort of vocab from this cretinous specimen.

"Pseudonyms?"

"Yeah, fake names."

"I know what the word means, pal. Don't get smart. It'll hurt, believe me."

"Yeah, well could be Cherry, Cuddles, Candy, Shandy, Stella. List goes on."

"Sounds like my little black book." I smiled, for my own enjoyment, not his. And it was true, my little black book was on volume two now.

He stared sullenly at me, nervously glancing at Betty in all her gunmetal glory. I kept her well-oiled and the sheen carried a certain cachet.

"So, Jakey, you remember her face."

"Yeah."

"And where do you think I should start looking for her?"

"Look, man, most of the girls who were working here have all gone to Danvers's brothel down the street."

Before I could ask anything else, Cindy stormed in.

"Okay city fucker, time's up. Off you fuck, now!"

I re-holstered Betty and walked back to the reception behind Cindy's large, waddling arse, as broad as two oxen. Yep, her backroom days on horizontal duty were as extinct as a dodo.

I got back to the front counter and stopped.

"I said out, fucker. I was watching you on the camera. How dare you point a fucking gun at my Jakey."

I put my hands on the counter and leant in a bit. "Look, Cindy, I wasn't going to hurt him. And it's licensed, I'm not a thug. I just want to find Courtney."

"I don't give a shit."

"Just give me an address and I'll be gone."

"You left-handed or right-handed?"

"What?"

"Which is it?"

"Ah…left." Always lie when you don't know what's around the bend.

Before I could even properly register the movement, a small wooden bat had emerged from under the counter, swung up and over in an arc, and smashed into the back of my left hand.

Fuck, more pain!

"What the fuck?" I yelled at her.

"Out now, fucker."

Jakey was standing at the entrance to the hallway, an oily grin on his rat face.

"If I see you again, fucker, it'll be torture time for you," I promised him.

He gave me the bird. I thought about pulling out Betty and letting a round go above his head. Would have given me a hoot, but then it would have made the girls on duty shit themselves, and that wasn't fair. It wasn't their fight.

"Fuck you both, you in-bred cunts." And I stormed out the door.

I rubbed my aching hand as I walked to my car. My rule of thumb about lying in the first instance had been bang on the money. Fucking bitch.

I got into my car around the corner and locked the doors. Around this bum-fuck town that seemed mandatory. Mind you, the prevalence of in-bred progeny here would indicate that there was plenty of fucking of the non-bum variety, too.

I pulled the half of Scotch from the glove box and took a stiff swig. I savoured the burn down my throat. I took two more.

Then I pulled out the photo of Courtney's boy, Archie.

"Where the hell are you, little one."

Another couple of swigs. I looked in the mirror. My visage had seen better days. It was turning into a face for radio. Perhaps I needed to stress my character more.

I looked back at Archie's picture.

"Well, little buddy, you sure as hell better be worth the paycheck."

If I ever got through this case with solving it, I suspected my paycheck would comprise of hours sampling each of Courtney's orifices. Still, I've definitely had far worse pay-days. And I could negotiate that wad of cash from her bedroom drawer.

Time to get back in the saddle, Jasper.

CHAPTER 9

Opalite was less than half a klick away. Its exterior lighting wasn't too loud, but along with the shuttered windows at the front it certainly made it clear that this was a house of pleasure for payment. The place looked pretty recently renovated, too, and no expense had been spared on the security cameras that lined the front eaves like a colony of bats.

I parked a few car lengths away: not too close to be obvious, but not too distant to prevent me legging it to my wheels if the necessity arose. And in my world it often did.

My head was starting to throb again so I grabbed the Nurofen from the glove box and washed a couple down with a mouthful of whiskey. I looked in the mirror. The gash on my head was looking a bit raw but wasn't bleeding. A couple of bruises were darkening nicely on my face. Guess I wasn't going to be pulling off any Brad Pitt impersonations this evening. Bugger it, Jasper, into the breach again, son.

I wandered back to the brothel and pressed the buzzer. A camera lens regarded me and then the door clicked open.

Yep, definitely a new refurbishment and pretty classy considering what a bumfuck town this was.

And the receptionist wasn't too shabby either. She certainly would do well out back too, if she wanted extra shifts. Generally, however, the receptionists were either hookers past their expiry date, like Cindy, or were girls who weren't prepared to lie on their backs for the extra rate of pay.

"Welcome to Opalite. I'm Svetlana. How are you this evening?"

"I'm okay, Svetlana. I like that name." Yeah, I'd happily do this one.

She stared at my battered head and face, probably giving me the appearance of a beaten mongrel. Well, not too far from the truth, really.

"You don't look really okay." Her accent was definitely Russian or Ukrainian.

"Don't be fooled by appearances, I've looked much worse before."

She smiled. "So, a lady to look after you?"

I smiled back. "Well, Svetlana, I didn't walk in here looking for the local book club, that's for sure."

"Smart arse." But she was still smiling, so all cool. "Preferences?"

"Brunette, slim, and very sexy."

"I only have one brunette working this evening, Angel. And all our girls are sexy, mister."

"I'm sure. I'll take Angel, then."

I handed over the cash she demanded.

Then she picked up the phone, looked at me, and said something in Russian. I could hear a muffled male voice on the other end, and not speaking English. She said a couple more things and then hung up, mentioning Angel at the end. I figured she was tipping off the boss that a stranger was in the premises.

I took my directions and walked down the corridor past the quaintly named rooms: Fellatio Forum, Route 69, and mine, Cunnilingus Chamber. They knew me well. I wondered if the next door down was Anal Annex or similar. Like I said, quaint in that debauched brothel way.

I stepped inside the Chamber. It was a typical room for a reasonable class bordello: king-size bed, red satin sheets, lavender incense burning, subdued lighting from lamps, and well over-heated. Encouraged one to get naked, which was the general idea, really.

I sat down on the bed that was super comfortable. There was a bowl of condoms and lube tubes on the bedside table, along with the obligatory tissues.

I took my jacket and shirt off, tossing them on the chair next to the bed, and then lay back, my eyes closing as I considered eating some pussy.

I came to with a honey-soaked voice saying, "Wakey, wakey."

I opened my eyes and I'd swear it was a sexy Helen of Troy standing there, although in raunchy lingerie that those lusty Trojans probably hadn't imagined let alone invented. It wasn't Courtney, alas.

"Bloody hell, you are stunning."

She giggled as she said, "Thank you", and then straddled me on the bed, leaning down and kissing me on the lips. She tasted of berries.

"I didn't think you were allowed to kiss the clients."

"That's just something we working girls say when we don't want to kiss someone, which is often. But it's up to us."

"Lucky me, then."

"You're going to feel very lucky by the time I've finished with you, handsome."

She started rubbing my chest. Then she took of her skimpy bra and brushed her superb tits across my face. Jesus, I had to work hard in this job. My mind retuned to my task.

"Babe, as gorgeous as you are, you're not the one."

She lifted her chest off my face. "Excuse me?" She looked a mixture of confused and offended, understandably. I mean, even a gay priest would have thought twice before discouraging this stunner.

"I mean I'm looking for someone, that's all."

"Honey, I'm the best lay in this joint, and there is some stiff competition, so I don't think you quite know what you're talking about."

"I have no doubt you are sensational, but I'm not being completely honest."

She laughed a deep belly laugh. Her laughter made her body vibrate on top of me and my old fella started moving even more.

"Honey, come on, honesty in a brothel? That's like Easter eggs at Christmas, doesn't happen."

"I'm sorry, I'm looking for Courtney."

She wiggled down me a bit, rubbing her hand on my junk. When she undid my trousers, my cock, now as hard as steel, sprung forth from my boxer shorts.

"Oh, I do like the look of that, big boy." She peeled my trousers and shorts off. And the girl had class, she also took my socks off. "No self-respecting girl fucks a man still in his socks," she grinned at me.

My turn to laugh. "But I am looking for Courtney."

She peeled off her knickers and took a condom from the bowl.

"Shh." She wrapped my beast in latex and then slid her pussy over it. She started riding me. When I opened my mouth to say something, she put her finger on my lips and repeated, "Shh."

And, like her boast, she was a hell of a lay. The way she made her vaginal walls grip and massage my cock was something to behold. I've had some seriously great fucks in my life, but this was top-notch.

She started masturbating herself. "Now, honey, don't you dare come yet. I'll tell you when."

Oh, bugger, I was going to have to think of gross things to delay my libidinous explosion.

She was practiced and worked herself into a frenzy in moments. "Okay, honey, go for your life!"

As she started to buck with her orgasm, I blew my load. We both groaned aloud at the same time.

She flopped down on top of me. "Now, do you agree I am a fantastic fuck?"

"You are top shelf, baby."

She kissed me hard. "Thank you, handsome. Now, how do you know Courtney?"

It was a bit hard to switch mental focus given my waning cock was still inside her, but I concentrated. "Courtney's here? You know her?"

"Yes. But keep your voice down. I know her, but she's not here tonight."

"When, then?"

"Why are you looking for her?"

"It's a long story."

Her eyes drifted to my clothes on the chair and she suddenly tensed. I looked over. The butt of my Beretta was clearly visible from under the jacket.

"Ah, don't worry, it's licensed and so am I, private investigator."

"So, you're not a cop?"

"No. And I am a friend of Courtney's."

There was a bang on the door. A voice that sounded as if it belonged to a retarded ape said, "Time's up, unless you want to take him up to the spa bath."

"No, we're done, I'm finishing up. Thank you."

"When will Courtney be on next?"

"I'm not sure, but I'm going on holidays tomorrow, so I won't see her for a while."

"Fuck. Have you got a number for her or something?"

"Sorry, honey, I don't."

"Listen to me, babe, I have to find her."

There was a more aggressive bang on the door. The subnormal primate spoke again. "I said time's up! Unless you show me the bucks."

"Coming now," called Angel. She bent down to me. "Listen, I have to go."

"Fuck it, I'll pay more."

"No, you don't understand. That thug is there on my boss's instructions. The boss likes to do some shifts with the girls himself. Know what I mean?"

"Yeah. Okay, where can I maybe find Courtney?"

"She usually hangs out at the Lavender Pub on the highway out of town. You can't miss it."

"The Lavender Pub."

"Yep, on the highway."

"Thank you, you're a sweetheart."

She smiled, with a tinge of melancholy, as she stood up. As she turned to walk to the door, I jumped up off the bed and grabbed her arm. I pulled her close to me. I leant down and her lips raced up to meet mine. We swapped a litre of saliva in seconds.

She smiled at me. "Thank you, handsome. You make me feel like I want to be stalked by you."

"Baby, that's the first time a woman has said that. And I'd do so much more than stalk you."

And with that she was gone.

I sat in my car, exhausted and not sure what was throbbing more, my head or my cock. First World problem, I guess. I grabbed some more Nurofen and washed them down with some whiskey again. I checked the doors were locked, and leant back in my seat. I started drifting.

Images flashed.

I was at a bar. Not exactly unusual.

I was approaching a woman. Also far from unusual.

She had her back to me.

She turned as I touched her shoulder.

Stunning.

Courtney?

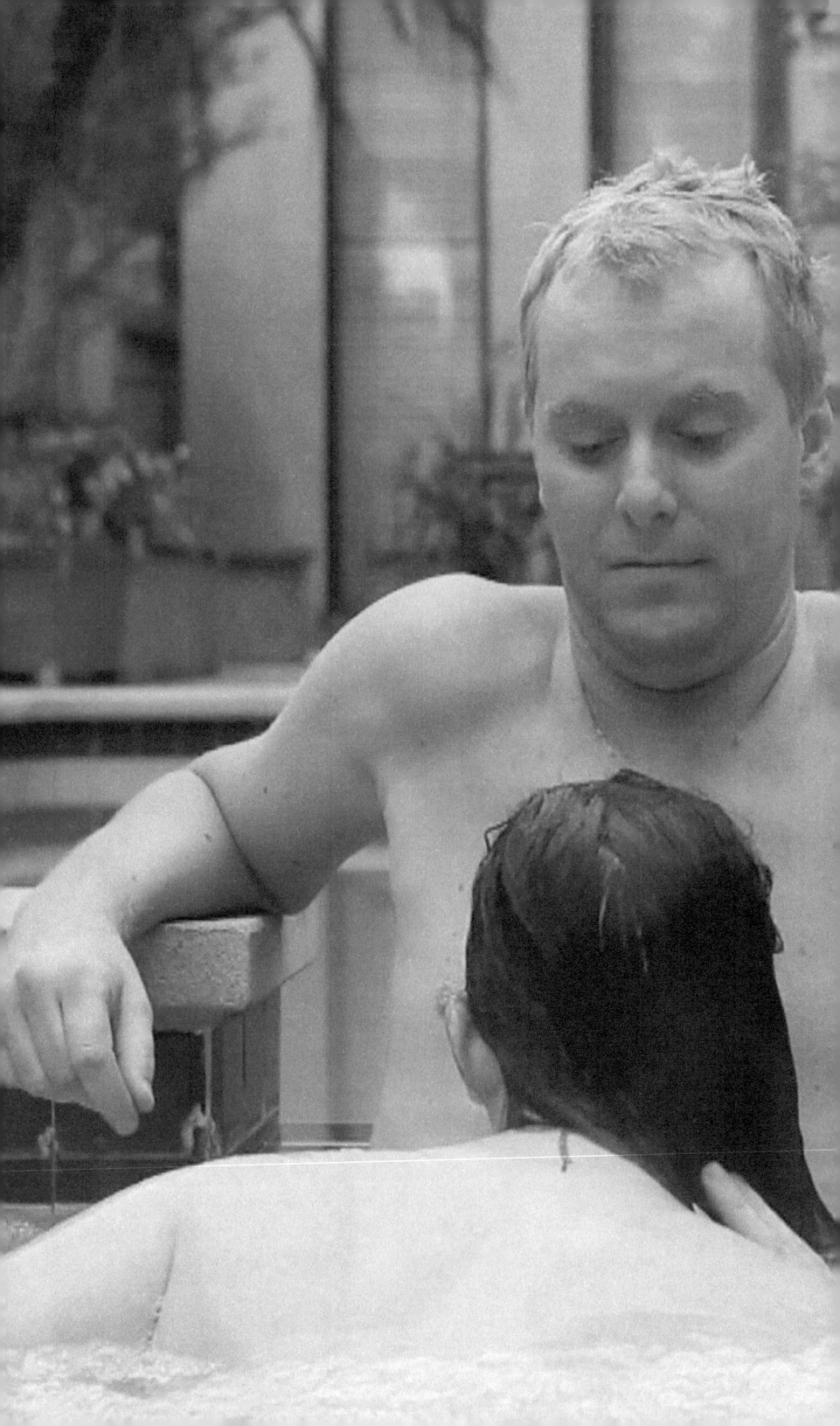

CHAPTER 10

I woke up still in my car and saw that a couple of hours had passed. I also saw that it was close to closing time for country-town pubs. Damn, back to work, Jasper boy. I hadn't intended the nap, but clearly my body was dictating its immediate needs. I looked up into the mirror. My bandaged head looked semi-reasonable. Well, it added character anyway. And going on the evidence it certainly wasn't lowering my prospects with the ladies. I couldn't remember a time my testicles had felt as drained as right now. I felt for Betty Beretta on my belt, always loved the reassurance, and started the car.

I pulled into the car park of the Lavender Pub in less than five minutes. The lights were still on in the front bar, although there were only two vehicles out the front. It was one of those typical country pubs that had seen its heyday decades ago and was now a pastiche of rusty corrugated iron, flaking paint, and sagging verandah timbers. The sign announcing its name looked bright and newish, but you know what they say about a pig and lipstick.

As I walked towards the front door, I spotted the reason for its name: a garden bed along the length of the front verandah dotted with mostly dead lavender bushes. Those that weren't already out of their misery were clinging to life amidst beer cans and cigarette butts. One of them even managed to sport a used condom from its twigs.

Before I stepped up towards the door, a bogan in uniform, being a checked flannel shirt and dirty jeans, stumbled out, putting his Akubra hat on, and belching loudly.

"G'day, mate, fucking better out than in." He grinned as he tripped down the three steps, and then steadied himself as he dug in his pockets for his car keys. Before he made it to his car, a dirty white Holden ute, he stepped over to the garden bed, unzipped his jeans, and let forth a torrent of steaming piss onto the botanical survivors.

He grinned inanely at me. "Like I said, mate, better out than in." It was about what I felt about him and the human race, but I didn't respond.

I mounted the steps and prepared myself for the local version of the Ritz Carlton.

The front bar was small, poorly lit, and about as lively as the lavender garden. As I walked to the bar, the last table occupants, two scruffy looking farm-hand types, stood up and waved at the barmaid, one of them calling out, "See you tomorrow, Trudes."

"See ya, fellas, drive safely," she said.

She turned to look at me.

"What can I get you, sugar?"

"I think I need a coffee. Any chance?"

She smiled. She was blonde and pretty in that skanky, titty-bar manner. And her bod and her rack would look stellar on a pole. "Yeah, I can rustle one up."

"Black and two sugars, please."

"No worries." She headed down to the coffee machine at the far end of the bar.

I turned the other way and there was a dark-haired woman sitting at the bar with her back to me. It looked as if she was reading a book in between sipping on a glass of white wine. She was the only customer left, as far as I could see.

Damn me. Same hair, same build.

"Courtney?"

She turned and looked at me. Cute as a bug's ear, but not Courtney.

"Hello." She gave a cheeky grin.

"Doesn't matter."

"Oh, okay." The smile evaporated.

Shit, I don't like upsetting the ladies, especially the good sorts.

"Look, sorry, I thought you were someone else."

She was half looking back at her book. "And who did you think I was?"

"Just this girl, doesn't matter."

"Whatever." She returned fully to her book.

Good one, Jasper, you idiot.

My coffee arrived and Trudes, presumably Trudy, gave the bookworm a look and wandered off.

I took a good sip and put my smokes packet on the counter.

Bookworm glanced at them, then over to me. "Going to offer me one?"

A reprieve loomed. "Of course." I held the pack open. She drew out a cigarette and I lit it for her. Then I did one for myself.

"Hi, I'm Jasper."

She giggled. "Funny name. I'm Ebony." With that she swivelled to face me and put her book down on the counter.

"Ebony? I like that name, it's cool."

She smiled and looked into my eyes. It was like facing a pair of dark-brown honey pots. Bet there'd been a few lads lured to destruction by those.

"Actually, Jasper is pretty cool, too. And never heard it around these parts."

"And seriously, from the back you did look dead set like the girl I'm looking for."

Trudy was back and rolled her eyes, pouring herself a wine and toping up Ebony's glass.

"Well, sorry to disappoint you," said Ebony.

"Honey, you are anything but a disappointment, you're stunning from the front."

Trudy groaned.

"Smooth, aren't you?" said Ebony.

I chuckled. "Mostly, I try to be, yeah. But I'm here to get a job done."

"Oh," she pouted, "and I thought you were looking for love."

She and Trudy cracked up laughing together.

Good looking girls get to take the piss out of me, anyone else cops a smack in the chops.

"Seriously, I'm a private investigator."

Trudy pointed at my now empty coffee cup. "Time for something stronger then, Mike Hammer?"

"Yeah, if you ladies feel like a couple of bourbons."

"Coming right up, fella."

"Cool. Just got to go drain the lizard, so sit tight."

I headed off towards the sign that announced the gents' bathroom.

I was just shaking off at the urinal when I heard the door squeak open. There hadn't been any blokes left in the bar, so perhaps Ebony was coming in for a bit of a pub toilet shag. Filthy, seedy jobs, but always memorable. I can always manage seedy, it's my middle name. I turned as I zipped up and there was this wiry bloke with sharp eyes and dressed too cleanly for this town. I smelt copper. Well, at least that meant I was less likely to get bashed again. He looked vaguely familiar.

He stood inside the door, blocking my exit.

"Quite the ladies' man, aren't you?"

"I try, mate."

"Got a question for you, Casanova."

"Do I need a lawyer, officer?"

He glared at me, looking pissed off I'd made him so easily. "Don't be cute, lover boy."

"Don't worry, you're not my type. Now, you had a question."

"Do you often hang out at illegal fight clubs?"

Ah, that was where I'd seen him: in the car outside the fight shed.

"No, mate, I'm just passing through town."

"Is that a fact?"

"Yes, it actually is. Why? You from around here? One of the local law?"

"Yes, I'm a cop, Jasper. Detective Barkly."

"So, you've done your checks on me."

"Your car rego. And I know you're a private dick."

"Well, maybe you can help me out then."

"You chasing Danvers?"

Yeah, wasn't sure I should let on my business exactly. I gave him a maybe look.

"Look, Jasper, I'm about the only legit cop left in this shitty town. Danvers has got to the rest of them, or at least the ones who aren't too lazy to do any police work."

"Corruption in the cops? Who'd have thought?" I grinned at him.

He didn't have any sense of humour.

"Listen smartarse, there's a big shipment coming in early tomorrow. I'm fucking sick of this crook who reckons he's untouchable. So, I'm going to bring him down. And I've got back-up coming up from the city, clean back-up."

He stepped forward and put his finger on my chest.

"So, Jasper Clay, I don't want your business interfering in my business. Is that crystal clear?"

I nodded at him. "I'll try not to get in your way."

"You'd better not. Or I'll use your PI licence to wipe my arse next time I take a dump. And I'll be sure to have a good curry first."

Could have told him I was retiring, but didn't think that would be very constructive in the current situation.

"Good luck with Danvers, officer."

He glared at me, turned and walked out.

Back in the bar, Ebony had disappeared. Trudy was cleaning glasses behind the bar.

"Where's Ebony?"

"Guess she got tired of waiting, mate. Or maybe she thought that other guy coming in and following you to the dunny meant you played for the other team."

"Fuck me, if there's one sure thing in my life, it's my love of pussy. Believe me."

She put two shot glasses on the bar and filled them with bourbon.

"Well, mate, perhaps it's Ebony's loss, then. We can play instead."

She tossed her shot back and refilled it. I followed suit.

"I'm Trudy. And I like to party, if you know what I mean."

"I'm Jasper, and I've been known to party myself."

"I'm closing up. Wanna come down the back room with me and drink?"

"Hell, yes!" I was thinking about getting invited to come down her back passage. She looked as if she'd be an anal artisan. But all in good time.

Trudy sat me on a tattered old couch and flicked the switch on a stereo stack unit. She poured us more shots and she knocked back three in quick succession. She was still standing and I'd been hoping to be getting touchy-feely on the couch by now. Then she took another shot and handed me the bottle. She started to gyrate to the music and damn she could move those hips. She was smiling in that pouting way and she kept looking at me through now heavy-lidded eyes. She hadn't been wearing much to start with, but what there was came off one piece at a time. When she was down to her lace knickers, she dropped to her knees in front of me, reaching for my zipper. I was barred up already and definitely ready for a blow job. I leant my head back on the couch and awaited hot lips around my cock.

Nothing happened. The music was still beating, but Trudy wasn't.

I looked down and touched her face lying against the inside of my thigh. She snored ever so slightly.

For fuck's sake! So near…

I gently rocked her shoulder, but she was out for it. Clearly you needed to get Trudy active before the fourth or fifth shot. If only I'd known.

Okay, Jasper, you miss out on this one, son. As much as I would have liked to have wanked myself off over that lovely face, sleeping or passed-out girls are over that non-consensual red line.

I slid my leg out from under her and lowered her head onto the couch. I swallowed some more bourbon and I headed out.

I opened the locked front door to liberate myself from the bar and before I could even step onto the verandah, my way was blocked by three dudes standing there. It was Brodie with a pair who looked like the two thugs who'd taken Courtney, and the same pair from the fight club: Fat Ralph and Slim. Fuck, this town was non-stop.

"Evening, gentlemen." I didn't mean either word.

None of them said anything, just glared at me. Slim had that cosh in his hand. I didn't feel inclined to meet that again.

"What? You expecting me to buy you a drink? Oh, so sad, the pub's closed." I smiled at them.

Brodie opened his slimy mouth. "You need to take a hint, fella. Leave our town tonight."

"Brodie, you little shit, I was hoping not to see you again."

"And I ain't wanting to see you again, ever, full stop. Leave town. This is Danvers's town, and the likes of you are not welcome. And as for Miss Courtney, she is owned by the man. Now fuck off."

"What do you know about Courtney?"

Fatso grunted. "You fuck too many women, boy."

"Well, looking at you, mate, I'd guess four legs was more your style."

"Funny cunt. You heard the man. Take off or it might be your last night alive."

"Really? I was just starting to enjoy Elmore. There are lots of lovely women who all seem to want some city meat. Guess the fact that I wash and have only got five fingers on each hand gives me an advantage."

Slim and his cosh took a step towards me.

I whipped out Betty. The 9mm barrel had the desired effect. The forward lurching rock-ape did a fancy two-step back movement.

"Yeah, didn't think so. Why don't you all fuck off. And by the way, Ralphy, that Cuddles was one hot fuck."

Fat Ralph pointed his finger at me. "You're a dead man."

They all backed off and walked over to a hotted-up Falcon. I watched the taillights disappear and could still smell the acrid, burnt-rubber smoke as I turned back into the bar, hearing some movement behind me.

I saw a mane of blonde hair, not Trudy's, behind the flash of something red coming my way.

"No, wait…"

Then I realised the red was the fire extinguisher, just in the millisecond before it hit me and my lights went out.

I heard two female voices, one of them Trudy's.

"What the hell, Sam?"

The other girl spoke. "I came in the back way to find you and saw this dude standing at the doorway. Then I saw the gun, so I thought he was robbing the place and might have hurt you. I just reacted and hit him with the first thing I could find."

"You're a sweetheart, but I was going to fuck him, you know my special routine, but then I fell asleep."

The other girl's voice got closer. "You think he's all right, Trudes? Should we get him to a doctor?"

"Maybe. You could take him for a check-up after you drop me home. I'm shattered, babe, so I need my bed."

"He is a bit of a looker, isn't he."

"Yep," said Trudy. "So much better than the local offerings. He was in the bar trying to crack onto Ebony, but ended up with me."

"Help me get him to the car."

I still wasn't feeling very communicative as they half-dragged half-carried me out the back door. They bundled me onto a back seat and I went out again.

CHAPTER 11

I was drifting in and out lying on the back seat as Sam drove. At some point the car stopped and Trudy got out. Then the car moved again and I woke up as it came to a stop down a side driveway to what had to be the biggest fuck-off mansion in this shitty town.

I half-stumbled in a side door with Sam holding me up, although I was starting to get a clearer head. Next thing I knew was being guided into a bedroom, clearly a girl's room judging by the bright pastel colours and the girl pop star posters on the wall.

Sam sat me down on the bed and took my jacket off. She turned on a lamp and closed and locked the door.

She put her face close to mine. "Yeah, as if I'm going to take this piece of man meat to a hospital. You're going to get treated by Nurse Samantha instead."

I thought I was conscious, but who knows. It was getting hard in this town to sort out reality from dreams, or nightmares.

Talking of getting hard, something else started to as Sam brushed her hand along my crotch. She was blonde, skankily pretty, and young. Maybe too young. But I'd never been described as a piece of man meat before. Oh well, first time for everything. And whatever her age, it sure as shit wouldn't have been Sam's first time. She would have had trouble even remembering her virginity. In fact, I doubted she'd even be able to spell the word.

She licked my face. "You need a shower, honey?"

I mumbled and shook my head. I just wanted to rest.

"Well, I'm going to have a quick one, a shower that is, and then be back in a minute to give you a rub down and other treatment that hunky bits of man meat need."

She disappeared into an en suite bathroom and I heard the shower start as I flopped back onto the bed. It was super comfortable and I could smell her on the pillows.

I closed my eyes, but more to try and focus my brain than to sleep.

Before I could think too much, she was back, wearing only the skimpiest of knickers and her naked breasts moving towards me magnificently.

"Sit up, my man meat, and get that shirt off. And then lie on your front."

I've never been a guy to disobey a gorgeous near-naked woman, and I didn't see any reason to change my habits now.

Sam gave a great back and shoulder massage, and she bent down regularly, her hard nipples rubbing along my shoulder blades.

After a few minutes of that bliss, she rolled me over and sat right on my crotch, grinding her pussy against my cock, which all things considered was rising to the occasion admirably.

She grabbed my hands and planted them on her tits, which were the size of grapefruits and similarly firm. Then she bent down and stuck her tongue so far into my mouth I almost choked.

Then there was a knock on the door.

A deep male voice. "You in there, Sam?"

"Oh, shit," she whispered in my ear. She sat back up on me and reached for a shirt.

"Samantha?"

"Yes, Dad, I'm here. But I'm not dressed."

"You sleeping?"

"Well, I was! Can we talk in the morning, please Dad?"

"All right. Good night."

"Night, Dad."

She got off me and grabbed a bowl with weed in it from the bedside table. She started rolling a joint.

Bugger me, what the hell was going on here? And the dad bit worried the fuck out of me.

"How old are you, Sam?"

"Are you serious?" She looked highly offended.

"Hello, yes, I bloody am."

She grinned as she rolled the joint. "Relax, man meat, I am legal. Only just, but legal."

"So where am I? This your parents' house?"

"Yep, well my dad's really, Mum's dead. Anyway, you should feel privileged." She licked the paper completing the spliff.

"Privileged? How do you figure that, young lady?" And I definitely doubted any aspect of the lady label.

"Well, first up, you're about to fuck something young, hot and wild. Second, you are in the richest house in town, the Danvers residence. My Dad owns this town."

My head was clearing real fast now.

"Did you say Danvers?"

"Yeah." She lit the joint and took a well-practiced drag.

"So, Danvers is your father?"

"Yeah. That's the general idea of a dad, isn't it?"

"Shit."

"You know him?"

"Only by reputation, so far."

It was time to get out of here. Danvers's goons had already made it clear they wanted to hurt me, and I winced at the thought of how slow and painful they'd make it if I was caught chock-a-block up his daughter.

I started grabbing my clothes. The photo of Archie fell out on the floor. I scooped it up.

As I got dressed, my brain flashed back to a bar, a woman.

Sam was looking confused as she drew on her joint. The sweet smell of weed was filling the room.

"I gotta disappear, young lady."

"I'm not a lady, okay, so stop calling me that."

"Yeah, and in different circumstances I'd like to stick around and make you even less of a lady. But not here."

"Are you one of those city gay boys?"

I laughed and put my hand on her cheek. "So not gay. I'm actually the state president of the pussy appreciation society."

She raised her eyebrows. "There is such a thing?"

71

"Absolutely," I lied. "See you." Well, if there were, I would be a walk-up start for its leader.

I closed her door behind me and looked both ways down the hallway I found myself in. Fifty-fifty really. I could see the tops of staircases in both directions. I turned right and crept along the corridor. From the top of the stairs, I could hear music coming up from below. Down I went, as the exits had to be on the lower levels.

I moved along another passageway downstairs. The music and male voices were coming out of a room on my right. I tiptoed past its closed door and looked into the next doorway, which was open. It was a film projection room. I ducked in and peered through the glass portal in the wall. The room with the noise had a screen on the far wall, but it was in darkness. What was brightly lit up was a naked girl doing a pole dance on a small stage to the side of the film screen. She was hot. There were the three goons, including Brodie, necking beers and making boorish comments to the stripper. In a big armchair sat an older, brutish-looking man with a shaved head and neck tattoos. He was smoking a fat cigar and drinking whiskey or bourbon, judging by its colour. The main man from the fight club. So Club D was Danvers.

He pointed at the three goons. "Oi! Stop blocking my view."

"Sorry, boss," said one of them.

"And have you clowns sorted that city snooper out?"

They looked at each other, clearly not sure what lie they should tell.

Brodie spoke up. "Boss, we scared him real good. He got the message, so don't reckon we'll be seeing him in Elmore again."

"Well, I fucking hope not."

A door in the wall opposite the pole dancer opened and in stepped Sam. She was wearing a bath robe.

Danvers clicked his fingers at the stripper who turned the music off and scampered out the door Sam had entered through.

Danvers turned to Sam. "What the hell are you doing down here? I thought you were in bed?"

"Well, Dad, I was. But I had a man friend with me, from the pub, and he suddenly took off. You haven't seen him, have you?"

"Who is he?"

"Just some city dude. Good looking. Nice change from the guys around here." She sneered in the direction of the goons.

"Some city dude? Don't suppose he had blond hair and a gun, did he?"

"So, you have seen him?"

"For fuck's sake!" bellowed Danvers, putting his head between his hands, knuckles straining white over his bald head.

He looked back up at the now silent room. He pointed at the goons. "Okay, clown team, how about you get out there and find this fucker, and then bring him to me. And don't fuck it up this time, clear?!"

The three stooges nodded obediently.

Time to get the fuck out of here, Jasper.

CHAPTER 12

I scooted along two more corridors in this labyrinth from hell trying to find an exit. I saw what looked like an exterior door, judging by the deadlock in the inside, and headed for it. Shit, it was deadlocked. If I didn't escape pronto, I wasn't going to be man meat, I was looking at dead meat.

Then I heard some sobbing. Always the sucker, Jasper.

I followed the plaintive sound and pushed open a door that was slightly ajar. A young woman was sitting on a bed. She was wearing a slinky black lingerie number and her body was stellar. I couldn't see her face as her head was hanging down as she cried.

She must have sensed my presence. "Listen, can you give me a bit longer? I'm still tired."

That voice. I moved towards her. "Courtney?"

She looked up then, her face beautiful despite the dark runs of mascara mixed with tears.

"Babe, if only you knew what I've been through to find you."

"Jesus! Jasper?"

She stood up.

"No, Jesus." I smiled at her and managed to get one in return. I stepped up to her and put my hands on her shoulders.

She ran her fingers over my various head injuries.

"What happened?"

"Like I said, what I have been through."

"Seems so long ago since our 'love can be found in the arms of a stranger' moment."

"Sure does, babe."

My synapses fired and memories floated back. My mind flashed back to that high-class bordello, the stunningly gorgeous and wanton Courtney, and the wild lovemaking. And then her whispering in my ear that it was rare to find love in the arms of a stranger. It was one of my most memorable nights, from a rich tapestry, you understand.

Back to the present. And the present danger.

She kissed me and then looked into my eyes. It was like being sucked in by two stunning whirlpools. "When I hired a private investigator, I didn't expect you to turn up, wasn't even sure it was you until you arrived. And then Danvers took me. He's been keeping me a prisoner here. I even had one of his thugs take me to and from the parlour today. I couldn't try to escape because he has my son, Archie."

"Yeah, the handsome little fellow. I've still got the photo." I tapped the outside of my jacket pocket.

"Oh, Jasper, what are we to do?"

"Babe, I don't know what it is about you, but I think I've fallen for it. Again."

"Bet you say that to all the girls." She grinned.

"No, actually I don't. Falling for them is not my usual style. Now, Courtney babe, we have to get the hell out of here."

Her eyes darted behind me in the split second before she yelled, "Look out!"

I felt the blow to the back of my head and down I went. Lights out.

CHAPTER 13

Whatever my cheek was lying on felt cool and smooth, like rubber or vinyl. My eyes didn't want to open, but a load of ice-cold water hit my face and made up my mind for me.

In front of my face, I could see some black boots. Above me I could hear laughter. I pushed myself up with my hand so I was lying on my side. I was in a boxing ring and I guessed it was the one in the fight club I'd peeked in on earlier.

I saw Brodie's slimy smile, then the other two goons, Slim and Fatso Ralph. What the fuck Cuddles saw in him was so far beyond me it hurt to contemplate. Must have been hung like a fucking donkey or something.

The trio parted and Danvers stepped forward.

He looked down at me. "Do you know where you are?"

"Ooh, let me see. A boxing ring?"

"Yeah, a funny cunt, aren't you?" His fist swooped down and belted me in the face.

Fuck, ouch!

He was standing over me now. "I don't know who you are, city boy. I don't know what sort of trip you think you're on. But I find you in my town, *my* town, stepping all over my fucking toes. You're fucking all my girls. *My* girls."

I laughed. "It's a good town for fucking."

Fat Ralph sunk his boot into my guts. "Yeah, you fucked my girlfriend, arsehole."

Danvers resumed. "I find you fucking my daughter and getting her stoned."

Damn, lying here now I wished I had fucked Sam.

"Ah, no…"

"Shut up! And now to top it off you want to take one of my girls, Courtney, one of my very best. And by the fucking look of you, you can't afford her."

He motioned to Slim. Out came that fucking cosh and he jabbed it hard into my guts.

Fuck me, I was over the beatings. I really should have fucked his daughter while it was on offer, and up the arse. I'd put money on young Sam not being an anal virgin either.

I laughed at him again.

"Yeah, it's so funny isn't it, mate? This is my fucking business you're messing with. And now, here, this is just business, too."

He punched me in the head twice.

I shook my head to clear my thinking again.

Seeing all this testosterone polluting one room was suffocating. There were more male hormones flowing than in a game of soggy biscuit. I mentioned that toxic male parlour game to a date one night. Well, she was broad-minded, she was a paid date. But whilst she'd been delightfully open-minded in entertaining my lustful desires, she'd never heard of soggy biscuit. So, I explained.

My narrative climax, excuse the pun, was, "And the last ejaculator gets to eat the biscuit."

"Yuk!"

"What, you've never had more than one bloke's gism in your mouth?"

She giggled. "Of course I fucking have. But I don't eat biscuits. Girl in my line of work has to watch her figure, you know."

It had been my turn to laugh.

I looked back up at Danvers and smiled at him. "A man's gotta do what a man's gotta do."

"Oh yeah, sure thing, funny man. So now it's your turn to get fucked up, but not by us."

He stepped back and the goons did likewise.

One of them lifted the top rope and a chick, one of the fighters I'd seen, stepped into the ring. Danvers stepped out, followed by his henchmen.

"What the fuck?" I groaned.

"Meet Sara, our champion," said Danvers, sitting down in a canvas director's chair ringside. The goons lined up behind him, like some guard of honour from *Planet of the Apes*. "You like the girls, pretty city boy, so try this one for size."

Sara was certainly fit. Her face was a bit hard, not helped by the sucking-a-lemon expression, but she had a great body. Put it this way, I wouldn't kick her out of the bed if she farted. But I figured this was not the right place or the right time to be putting the hard word on her. Most worryingly, she was swinging a heavy chain in her hand. That looked anything but sexy.

I looked over at Danvers and pointed at Sara. "You want me to fight her?"

"You wanna get out of here alive, dipshit?"

"Wouldn't mind."

"Best you get up on your fucking feet then."

"Really?"

"This isn't multiple choice, dickhead."

"And if I decline?"

"Get up, shit-for-brains. Fight for your life, 'cos that's exactly what's on the line here."

I hauled my sorry arse vertical and staggered a bit as the blood rushed. Sara was bouncing on the spot, evidently keen to give me a flogging. I slipped my hand inside my jacket. No Betty on my belt, just the empty holster. Well, of course. I looked over at Danvers.

He was grinning, waving Betty around in his hand. "Well, hello!"

He handed my Beretta to one of the goons. "So, now we're all buddies around here, just who the fuck are you, shithead?"

I looked at him, considering my answer to that. "I'm the father of Courtney's child."

He groaned and rubbed his forehead. He turned to Sara. "Fuck him up!"

Bugger, this was going to hurt. I didn't want it to be my last appearance in the land of the living, but the odds were not looking flash.

I slid my jacket off and looked at Sara. At least she'd dropped the chain, but her fists were up and ready.

"Come on, then, let's do this, baby." I couldn't help a bit of bravado.

She didn't crack a smile. Guessed she only grinned when she was inflicting pain. Which was going to be any moment now.

She moved like lightning and her right fist socked into my jaw. That fucking hurt, but it was only the teaser I suspected.

I tried to take a couple of swings, but I may as well have been clutching onto a Zimmer frame compared to her speed. She ducked and weaved and two more punches hit my face and head.

The testosterone-soaked gorillas were hooting from the sidelines.

She made the most of my dazed look and came in real close and headbutted me.

I was staggering now.

The hooting got louder.

Then a roundhouse swing from hell just about took my head off and down I went, back onto the canvas.

Something was floating in my mouth. I spat a mouthful of bloody saliva onto the canvas, along with a tooth.

Danvers roared laughing. "That was nasty! Get up and fight, you weak prick."

I made it onto one knee.

Sara leant down towards me. "Come on punk, come and get some more of my special brand of loving."

I staggered to my feet. Being Jasper, I couldn't help myself. "Well, baby, any time your hard-arse pussy is available, I'll fuck it into the middle of next week."

Her foot came up and launched into my guts. I reeled back against the ropes and now had nowhere to retreat to. I took two more kicks and another punch to the head and down I went again.

She leant over me. "And you're such a pussy that I reckon you could fuck yourself."

I stayed in the prone position on the canvas. I sure wasn't in a rush for more punishment from the warrior wench. I could feel the wet patch under my cheek from my drool and blood. All class today, Jasper. And looking pretty fucked about now.

I was wondering what variety of pain would happen to me next when a phone rang from somewhere in the troop of apes next to the ring.

One of the goons said, "All good."

I heard a truck's loud reversing beeper outside and then watched as two of the goons walked over to the roller door and one of them started pulling on the chain to raise it.

Everyone seemed to lose interest in me, so I just lay doggo to watch proceedings and try to figure out a plan.

The roller door clattered up and then a flatbed truck with a shipping container on its tray backed into the opening a couple of metres and stopped.

I caught a glimpse of movement from Danvers and saw him motion to the goons now standing at the back of the truck. He handed something small to Brodie who went over to the truck, handing the object to fat, greasy Ralph. It was a key. Fatso undid the two padlocks securing the door latches on the container.

Slim lofted the latch bars and swung the doors open.

I saw half a dozen young female faces squinting as the light hit their eyes. They were all bound at their wrists and ankles. From where I was looking, three of the prisoners were almost certainly Thai girls, one looked Eastern European, and the other two were possibly Chinese or Korean. Shit, not only was Danvers running brothels and this town, he was a human slave trader, too. Fucky ducky! So this was the shipment that Detective Barkly had mentioned.

My battered brain was endeavouring to fire on all cylinders with this new development. One thing was immediately clear, despite my foggy frontal lobes: now I'd seen this, Danvers would not be letting me live, even if I vanquished the she-cat from hell, who was now standing at the ropes watching events.

No, I had to move, and do it fast.

Sara didn't see me lift my head up to look around. I saw a door over to the side, about five metres from the boxing ring, with no one in the intervening space.

I started to haul myself up.

And then everything happened really fast.

"Police! Police!" was being yelled and I could hear pump-action shotguns being cranked up. The place was filling up with armed visitors. Barkly, the cop from the pub toilet was in the lead, his service Glock levelled at Danvers. Other coppers were armed with Remington pump actions and Heckler and Koch assault rifles.

As I stood, the detective looked over at me.

"I didn't expect to see you again, mate."

"Well, Detective Barkly, the job wasn't finished. But I can promise you it'll be the last time. I'm through with this fucking in-bred shithole of a town."

He turned back to Danvers who yelled, "Fuck you, pigs!"

Everybody started yelling then, turning the place into a veritable swimming pool of testosterone. Not my scene, time to exit stage left. And to try not to get caught in the crossfire.

I took a step towards Sara who turned just as I launched my toecap full force into her crotch. Her eyes just about popped out of their sockets as she clutched at her pussy and collapsed on her knees. I'd read somewhere that a kick in the vagina was just as effective as one in the gonads. Never had cause to find out before if it was true, but seemed like my fact-checking was duly completed. Well, of course I'd never done it before. A pussy has multiple attractive uses, but not for kicking. Kissing, licking, fingering, fucking, even fisting, in a strictly non-violent sense you understand. But not kicking. And I know, because I'm a connoisseur of the steaming valleys of heaven. As I said, PI should stand for pussy inquisitor. Alas, poor Sara had earned Jasper's first cunt-kick.

I clambered out of the ring and made for the side door as the yelling continued.

As I emerged into the sunlight, a couple of shots were fired.

CHAPTER 14

There was an unmarked cop car at the corner of the building with a female leaning against it. Great body, radiant smile, and the Glock on her belt was sexy. I hadn't seen Detective Vanessa Tate for years. And back then I'd seen all of her, up close and personal. That night was in my connoisseur memoirs.

She smiled at me as I approached her.

"Jesus Christ, it's Sharon Tate back from the dead."

"Ha ha! Must be at least three years since that night of delicious depravity, Jasper."

"Yeah. You never returned my message."

"Sorry, honey, I'm a bit of a one-night girl. Don't take it personally, you are one of the best cunning linguists I have ever encountered."

I smiled at her. "Thanks for the compliment."

"Oh, the pleasure was all mine. Now, you need a ride, Jasper? And I mean of the business variety."

I laughed. Shit my ribs hurt. "That'd be awesome."

"Don't worry, we've got Courtney in a safe place."

"Really?"

"Yeah."

"Well, come on, take me to her."

"Get in, Lothario."

Ten minutes later we pulled into the car park of a nature reserve just outside town. There was another cop car there with two uniformed guys leaning against it.

Tate waved at them and pulled to a stop at the head of a path heading into the bushland.

"All right, Jasper. They're straight down that path. Courtney's taken the little boy outside to get some sun, he's been cooped up for ages."

I nodded at her.

"So, you've got fifteen minutes, then we'll need to get her to the station for her statement. I'll wait here for you."

"Thank you."

* * *

I walked briskly down the track, at least as fast as my battered body would allow.

I saw Courtney sitting on a rock next to a small lake.

As my feet crunched the gravel behind her, she turned around.

"Jasper!"

She stood up and stepped in front of me.

"God, Jasper, every time I see you, you've got a new bruise or cut."

She went to hug me. My ribs protested.

"Ouch!"

"Ooh, sorry."

"Tell me about it, love hurts."

Little Archie ran out from behind a bush, carrying a stick he was playing with.

"Jasper, this is…"

I put my finger to her lips to stop her there.

Archie came over, with that look of innocent curiosity on his face.

I crouched down in front of him and smiled.

"Hello, little man."

Courtney was beaming at us both. Perhaps she was fantasizing about happy families in the suburbs. Maybe that was what my retirement from the PI business destined me for. Maybe.

True to his photo, little Archie had my eyes.

EPILOGUE

Three months later, Samantha Danvers was sitting in her room at her aunt's house. She was living there now that her dad's property had been impounded as proceeds of crime.

Danvers himself was in remand awaiting trial, along with Slim. Fatso Ralph and Brodie had died in the shootout with the cops at the fight club.

Samantha was sitting at the dresser putting on her war paint before heading to the pub to seek out some horizontal solace with some man meat.

Her phone rang.

She frowned at the "No Caller ID" on the screen.

She picked it up. "Hello?"

"Samantha?"

"Who's this?"

"It's Jasper."

"What?! Are you fucking kidding me?! How dare you call me!"

"Sam, I really have to talk to you."

"Are you out of your fucking mind?"

"I need information. I'm desperate."

"Fuck you, Jasper. You put my dad in jail, you son of a bitch. There's no way I'm helping you."

"Sam, Courtney's d…"

The following is
a short story included in
A.B. Patterson's
Harry Kenmare, PI
At Your Service

WANKERS

She had a rack that would've distracted a Catholic priest from the altar boys. My first client in a fortnight sashayed unannounced into my shitty, smoke-filled office just as I was pouring my first Jameson for the day. Well, it was just after eleven a.m. I nearly spilt the amber nectar. I was transfixed. She reached my desk and held out her hand.

'Carmen Garcia.'

I took her hand. Firm grip. I liked that in a woman. It spoke volumes.

'Harry Kenmare, Private Investigator at your service.'

'Good.' The siren's smile, combined with her rack, must have destroyed dozens of poor rogues over the years.

I smiled back and thought to myself that she wasn't calmin' anything. Quite the opposite in fact. But I kept that lame line to myself.

Carmen sat down and opened her blue Gucci handbag. Matched her magnetic eyes, but I guess she'd worked it that way. She pulled out a cigarette case and lit up. Then she extracted two envelopes: one slim, the other chunkier.

I liked chunky envelopes almost as much as melonious breasts. I was alternating my eyes between them, and the envelopes.

'Look at me, shamus. Perhaps you can play with these puppies later.' She heaved her chest out dramatically to make the point. Two actually. 'You've got some work to do first.'

'Of course. You have my undivided attention, Carmen.'

She slid a photo across to me from the fat envelope. I could see the delicious, filthy lucre stacked in there.

'My daughter, Solara.'

'Runaway?'

'Yes. Family misunderstandings. I won't bore you. But I want you to find her.'

'Bring her home?' I had to ask, but I always hated those runaway jobs. A male PI in his forties trying to persuade a young woman into a vehicle looked rather more sinister than it was. It risked unwanted intervention.

'No,' she said.

That surprised me.

'No, I'd like her home, but it has to be her choice. She's an adult, just.'

Bugger me. Progressive parent. Unusual.

'Cool. So what do you want me to do?'

She slid the slimmer envelope towards me.

'Find her. Then give her this and ask her to read it. That's all you have to do.'

I picked it up. It was sealed.

'Any leads?' I asked.

'Her best friend confided that she's doing naked dancing.'

Most mothers I'd met would be staring into their laps at this point, but not Carmen. I suspected she'd had a bit of exotic work experience herself.

'Pole dancing?' I asked.

'No. Apparently some place where you dance in a room on your own. Sounds a bit strange to me.'

Ah, yes. I decided not to get descriptive.

'I know the places. Strip shows without a pole.' I could be the master of understatement when required.

'I'll take your word for it,' she murmured.

She pushed the fat envelope over. I tried not to be too speedy in picking up Big Boy.

'Five grand up front for expenses,' she said. 'When the job is done, there'll be another five waiting for you.'

Yeah, I'd figured she waltzed in from the rich end of town. For them, money was no object when they wanted something. And they bought people the way they bought things. Capitalism, left unchecked: sordid and mercenary.

But, business was business. I sure as hell wasn't going to be changing society.

'So, I just rock up and give Solara this, then report back?'

The alluring smile again. I was hooked.

'Almost. But you must take a photo of Solara holding the envelope and send it to me. Then you come see me. Deal?'

'Deal.' I stood up, held my hand across the desk and we shook.

As she was still holding it, she smirked at me and ran her tongue along her bright cerise lips.

'And when you visit to collect your payment, there could be certain non-cash bonuses. I like detectives.'

I wanted to fuck her on my desk right now. But this lady knew her priorities, so even my deepest Kenmare charm would've been futile. I'd have to show some penile patience.

'I'll look forward to that, Carmen. You're a very beautiful lady.'

I always thought a compliment went down well, so it was obligatory behaviour in my books. Of course, in this era of slavish political correctness, I had come a gutser on occasion: been rebuked, and even slapped. What the fuck sort of world had we landed in where a bloke couldn't tell a woman she was beautiful?

Carmen smirked saucily. 'I'll take the compliment, Harry, but lose the "lady" description.'

She winked, blew me a kiss, and left my office.

My erection and I stood in stunned silence.

The following afternoon, I started with the wank tanks; what polite society referred to, in hushed tones, as peep shows. The street name is rather more accurate. I knew four main ones. The first three yielded nothing. Now, there's no such thing as an upmarket wank tank, but there are degrees of grubbiness. And I left the least grubby until last.

I walked down the dimly lit stairs to Voyeurs & Vixens. I pressed the buzzer and smiled at the camera. The secure door wasn't there to try and keep anyone out as such, since these businesses wanted all the visiting desperados they could get. It was simply a delaying mechanism for the occasions the coppers turned up. The rules said the shows could only have one girl performing alone; live sex was not allowed. Of course, girl on girl action was where the revenue lay. So the door delay meant a warning light could be flashed in the performance chamber and one girl could scamper swiftly out the back door, leaving one worked up tart to play with herself. And so that is what the coppers always got to see. Only they didn't have to pay.

The door clicked and I stepped into the dingy cavern beyond. I walked over to the customer counter. Gazza, the manager, and a regular information source and drinking buddy of mine, was sitting behind it. Gazza, formerly Sergeant Garry Dawes of the Australian Commando Regiment, was a minus a leg, several metres of intestines, and half his face. His disability and disfigurement didn't lead to massive employment options. He'd found out the hard way that the Australian government didn't give a rat's arse about him leaving his body parts by a roadside in Afghanistan. Especially since he opened his mouth about the fourteen dead schoolchildren who some scrotum in intel had determined were Taliban fighters hiding out. They'd locked him in a psych hospital when he came home, which probably fucked him up more than the Afghan arseholes. But with his habit of posting virulent, anarchic rants on the Internet, the government still hated him. Or so he told me repeatedly.

So now, his compo cut off, Gazza had to scrape a living in here. His twelve-hour shifts consisted of encouraging the girls to do as much dildo work as possible, preferably anal; great for business. Then cleaning up the booths every few hours: bucket loads of sodden tissues and cum trails down the walls from the lazy fucks who didn't bother with the Kleenex.

Yeah, Gazza was simply drowning in the gratitude of his country.

'How's it hanging, Gazza?'

'Badly to the left, Harry. The old Afghan gait.'

We both laughed. We did every time, never tiring of the joke.

I pulled out the photo of Solara, along with five hundred of my expenses money. Figured no informant deserved it more than Gazza. I slid the folded bundle across his counter, along with the photo.

'Jeez, you're exceptionally generous today, Harry. Thanks, mate.'

'Least I can do, brother.' I tapped the photo.

'Yeah, absolutely,' he said without blinking. 'I wouldn't forget her face, or those tits, or the arse. She's fucking smoking hot, that one.'

'Working here then?'

He laughed. 'Of course, mate. After that butt naked audition, I had to hire her. Started last week. She'll be on in a couple of hours.'

'Sweet. Unusual glint in those eyes, Gazza?'

'Yeah. She's one of those sympathy skanks. Blew me. It was great.'

'Good on ya, mate.'

Gazza's 'sympathy skanks' were the girls who listened to him about Afghanistan – how the Taliban had fucked up his sex life, along with everything else – and then felt sorry enough for him to put out.

I looked back at the photo of Solara and tried to picture her sucking my dick. Yep, that image worked. Mind you, so did that of her mother, and Carmen was a red-hot prospect.

I waved in the direction of the tanks.

'What's the talent like in there at the moment?'

'Pretty bloody good actually. Two Dutch backpackers. And what they won't do to each other isn't even in the sealed section of the Kama Sutra.'

'Yeah? Dutch, I've always thought they're a pretty liberated lot.'

He smiled. 'Take a look, mate. Expand your definition of "liberated". Those two will rip open the windmills of your mind.'

He gave me a bag of two-dollar coins.

I went into the nearest available booth, trying to breathe through my mouth to reduce the cloying smell of semen, fresh and stale. I put a small stack of coins on the shelf next to the window, ready to feed the machine. First coin into the slot and the shutter in the viewing panel clicked open. I peered through the glass.

Gazza wasn't wrong. Tulip and Daffodil, or whatever they were called, were eating each other out with more enthusiasm than a busload of refugees in a McDonald's. Judging by the toys and lube tubes laid out on the mattress next to them, the best was yet to come.

Another coin.

The voice in the tank to my left was pure primate, grunting like a rutting gorilla.

The music increased in tempo, and so did the pride of Holland. Tulip, without slowing her pussy munching, greased a dildo the size of my forearm and eased it into Daffodil's arsehole, driving it in at least twenty centimetres.

Another coin.

Daffodil's ecstatic howling at the anal intrusion was clearly a motivation for the ape next door who finally managed some humanoid language.

'You dirty fucking sluts, I fucking love you!'

Slap, slap, slap, slap, slap, GRUNT!

Who was it who said something about a hundred chimpanzees left alone with typewriters would eventually produce Shakespeare? Yeah, not sure, but monkey-man next door wouldn't be much help to them.

Still, the busty Dutch tarts had definitely been worth a look, they did have some talent.

Another coin, or ten. No point wasting the opportunity to enjoy some more girl-on-girl. After the anal adventures, they went face to face riding a double-ender, licking each other's juices off their mouths. Outstanding. I'm not sure that this was what the Australian Border Force, or Border Farce as we knew it locally, had in mind when they'd issued the girls' work visas. But I reckon they were far better suited to this line of work than they would be to their visa-designated fruit picking and farm work.

I silently bade them farewell, thanked Gazza, and headed out into the sultry, darkening evening to kill some time at a bar.

Two hours later, Gazza had introduced me to Solara and I was sitting in the change room with her. She was topless, and divine.

'Your mother sent me. She said there'd been some family misunderstanding. Guess her peace offering is in this envelope.'

Solara snorted. 'Bitch.'

'So what was the misunderstanding?' I asked, trying not to fixate on her full, pert breasts.

'Mum brings her new boyfriend home. He touches me up and suggests I join him and mum for a threesome. I don't call that a fucking misunderstanding.'

'See your point.'

Mind you, I could see the boyfriend's point as well: this was a mother-daughter combo to have wet dreams about.

'Yeah, so did he, the sick fuck. I kneed him so hard in his nuts he was on the floor for ten minutes. Mum tried to talk me around. So I told her to go fuck herself and packed my bag.'

'Fair enough. Well, she said to give you this and it would explain things. And I've got to get a photo of you with the envelope.'

She frowned at me.

'So I can prove I've done the job. I need to get paid, young lady.'

She smiled. 'Okay. Give me your phone and sit forward a bit. Hold the envelope.'

She manoeuvred behind me, her breasts perched on my right shoulder. With one hand she held my phone in front of us, and with the other she turned my head so the side of my face was pressed into her bosom.

'Hold it up, Harry.'

'It's up all right, babe.' I held the envelope under my chin. Flash.

We looked at the salacious selfie. I couldn't help laughing. It was a shot for my album all right. And she wore a wicked smile that said, 'Fuck you, mum.'

She gave me the phone back. I texted the photo to Carmen.

I woke up late the next morning. After meeting Solara, I'd lubricated my fantasies rather generously at the Emerald Bar.

I was getting dressed when the phone rang. I answered.

'G'day, Gazza. Everything okay?'

'Don't know, Harry. A couple of suss-looking guys been snooping around the front and back.'

'Mate, you run a wank tank. You attract suss guys like flies to shit.'

'These two are different. I'm getting a vibe, Harry. Reckon they might be government, coming for me.'

'Gazza, I'm sure the fucking government, as much as they are total wankers, have really lost interest in you by now.'

'Not that simple. Couple of things I haven't told you, mate. Can you drop in? Like soon?'

'Yeah, of course, mate. See you shortly.'

'Thanks, Harry.' He rang off.

I was inclined to put it down to Gazza's never-ending, although understandable, paranoia. His mind had become a quagmire of conspiracy theories. But he was a mate, and he'd asked for help. And true mates always answer the call.

I got on my way to Voyeurs & Vixens.

I pressed the buzzer at the front door, but to no avail, twice. Strange, I thought. I couldn't see anyone in the vicinity. Possible that Gazza had gone for a crap, if there were no customers.

I pulled out my phone and called him. It went to voicemail. Okay, that was more than strange; that was a warning sign. Gazza always had his phone, even in the crapper. I knew that from awful experience.

I legged it around the block to the back entrance in the laneway. The normally locked door was resting on its latch. I wished that I'd packed my .38; I had an ominous feeling about this. And my old gut instinct was seldom wrong. Not that I'd always listened attentively. My personal life bore a painful testament to that.

I slipped inside silently. I could hear Gazza's articulate defiance, 'Fuck you, cunts!'

Then another male voice, 'We'll see about that, arsehole.'

A loud smack of flesh on flesh. Then another.

I moved down the short corridor and found one of Gazza's girls, stark naked, hiding in the doorway to the performance chamber.

I lent in to whisper in her ear, trying not to get distracted by her delectable body.

'I'm Harry, a friend of Gazza.'

'Lissa,' she sighed in my ear. She smelt floral, and edible.

How many of them?'

'Two I saw.'

'Know who they are?'

'No. Never seen them before. But they've been hurting him.'

I moved stealthily forward. Then I saw Gazza in his wheelchair, blood running out of his nose and with cut lips. Two goons were standing over him.

I strode in fast.

'Takes a real brave cunt to hit a disabled bloke, especially with two of you. You fucking weak pricks!' I kept the forward momentum, readying my fists.

The pair of thugs turned. The one closest didn't have time to react before my fist slammed into his gut, right in the solar plexus. He doubled over and hit the floor.

I needed to take out the other one, but he was now ready for me. He blocked my first swipe and returned the favour, his fist smacking into my jaw. That hurt. I went in to wrestle him. Then over his shoulder I saw Gazza move on his wheels, a large hunting knife in his right hand. Whilst walking wasn't exactly Gazza's forte these days, there was nothing wrong with his well-muscled arms. He drove that shiny steel blade literally into the goon's arsehole. He shrieked and collapsed on his knees. I drove my fist into his throat and he keeled over.

'Behind ya!' yelled Gazza.

I spun and lowered myself as the other thug came at me. I needn't have worried.

Lissa's breasts moved magnificently through the air as she swung a fire extinguisher full force into the goon's head. The clunking sound was sickening. He dropped like a sack of shit and didn't move again.

The goon with the lacerated rectum was moaning on the floor. I grabbed his hair and belted his head into the edge of the counter until he passed out.

'You okay, Gazza?'

'Bit of claret, Harry, that's all. But they were only just starting, so bloody glad you turned up. And, Lissa, thank you, honey.'

'No worries, Gazza.'

'Yeah, top work, babe,' I added. 'Tough and sexy. Great combination.'

She smiled at me. 'Well, handsome, any time you're into paying, then I'm into playing.'

'I'll keep that in mind.'

She headed back to the girls' change room.

'So who are these fuckers, Gazza, and what did they want with you?'

'They didn't exactly introduce themselves, mate, but they'll be government arseholes. Wanted to impress upon me the need to keep my mouth shut.'

'Why now?'

'I put out a few new blogs last week. Obviously upset the good folks down in Canberra.'

'Mate, you need to be more careful.'

'I'm a bit past that stage, Harry. Here, take this.'

He pulled out a small cloth bag from under his counter and handed it to me.

'Mate, it's a hard drive with a whole lot of shit on it. Enough to destroy careers and maybe even bring down the government.'

'What do you want me to do with it?'

'It's only a matter of time, Harry. Something will happen to me, I'm in their sights. There's instructions in there. Promise me, please, mate.'

'Yeah, of course. But let's hope that won't be necessary.'

'It will, mate. Now we better sort out these fuckers.'

I went through their pockets. No wallets, phones, or anything identifying. One of them had a set of picklocks that I pocketed. Explained the back door.

'Nothing on them at all means spooks,' said Gazza.

'Or thugs hired by the spooks. Either way, government.'

'Any ideas? We can't exactly call the cops.'

I let my devious mind run wild.

'No, not as such, but thinking outside the square, yes we can. You got a small freezer bag and sugar?'

He frowned. 'Yeah, in the kitchen back there.'

I came back a minute later with a plastic snap-lock bag full of white sugar. I shoved it in one of the goon's inside jacket pockets.

'Gazza, your camera out back's the only one out there?'

'Yeah, no others. Just for watching on the monitor here.'

'Cool.'

I dragged both inert thugs out into the quiet back lane. I got Gazza's knife, wiped his prints off it, and took it outside. I wrapped the hand of the goon with the intact arsehole around the knife handle. I closed and locked the door behind me as I returned inside.

'Now call it in, Gazza. You saw two guys fighting in the lane with a bag of white powder and a large knife. That'll motivate the local constabulary.' I smiled at him.

He grinned. 'You're a class act, Harry.'

In less than two minutes, we watched on screen as three patrol units screeched into the lane. The cops tumbled out of their cars with guns drawn. The two goons, now semi-conscious, were dragged away.

On my way out, I got Lissa's phone number.

I called Gazza the next morning to check he was okay. The conspiracy theories had come to visit early today: he was convinced more government enforcers would be on their way for him. I wondered what was on that hard drive. Was it something earth-shattering or was it a confection of Gazza's fucked up realities? I'd read the instructions: details about loading it onto the Web if Gazza disappeared or died. More paranoia, no doubt. But then, those hoods yesterday were the real deal.

Gazza said he was off to a public rally this afternoon. The Defence Minister and the Minister for Veterans' Affairs were making a public address about the issues facing returning vets, in particular the spiralling suicide rate that was getting some traction in the media.

Not before bloody time, I thought.

'Gazza, that's sure to be a complete pile of insincere garbage. Why are you bothering?'

'Mate, I want to give those fuckers a piece of my mind. Bit of good old-fashioned town square heckling.'

'Fair enough, have fun.'

'Oh, I will, Harry. You've no idea. As a great man said, let your plans be dark as night and when you move, fall like a thunderbolt.'

'Sun Tzu, if my memory serves.'

'Spot on. Anyway, mate, thanks for everything.'

'No worries, catch you soon.'

'Yeah. See ya, Harry.' He hung up.

My gut feeling twitched. Badly.

After lunch I flicked on the TV in my office to the twenty-four hour news channel. After a few headlines they crossed live to the veterans' rally. The two ministers were standing on a small platform taking it in turns to melt the microphones with the hot air of their patronizing pontifications.

Fuck, I hated the political class.

Then the camera angle changed to show more of the crowd, who were very vocal in jeering the politicians.

I saw Gazza in his wheelchair. Given his infirmities, other vets had given him space at the front of the crowd, along with two other chair-bound men. Gazza's wheelchair had a folded beach umbrella attached to its side, looking like a flagpole. That seemed a bit odd, given there was no rain forecast. And since Gazza was sitting in the blazing sunshine, he clearly wasn't interested in it as a parasol either.

Gazza was certainly getting into the heckling, and if the frequency of the word 'wankers' being shouted by him was anything to go by, the pair on stage must have been the record holders for ministerial masturbation.

Then the question time started, and Gazza was on the front foot, asking the ministers why his compo had been cut off. The politicians clearly knew his case, as they both gave banal answers using his name.

But that was as far as question time got.

I watched, stunned, as Gazza reached into the folds of his beach umbrella and pulled out an M16. He wasted no time. Butt to his shoulder, two quick bursts of automatic fire left both ministers dying on the stage.

My mouth was still hanging open as Gazza turned the rifle, swallowed the muzzle, and pulled the trigger one last time. The top of his head exploded off in a shower of blood.

I swallowed two stiff drinks and sat in melancholic, smoky silence at my desk.

What a fucked up world.

Even if I'd been trying, I couldn't have felt any sympathy for the dead politicians. They were all self-serving wankers who were interested in power and privilege, and who were quite happy to fuck Joe Citizen up the arse.

I read Gazza's notes again and got on the phone to my offsider, Trev. He did all my techo stuff.

He arrived forty minutes later and started fiddling on his laptop with Gazza's hard drive plugged in to it.

'It's not that hard, Harry, you fucking Luddite. You gotta get with the age, brother.'

'Mate, I'm from a different age. And I've got my skills.'

'Your predominant talents, aside from being a good detective occasionally, are drinking and fucking.'

'And the problem is?'

'Just saying.'

'Mate, the only problem is that there's no Olympic event for either. If there was, in this sport-obsessed country I'd be a fucking national hero.'

Trev just laughed.

We then watched in silence the surreptitious footage from Afghanistan: an Australian commander giving the orders; some of the soldiers hesitating; soldiers being yelled at and threatened; called cowards.

Then the onslaught of firepower.

All the bloodied bodies of the school kids and their teacher.

The panicked orders from the officers starting the official cover-up.

And on went Gazza's pseudo-documentary with secretly recorded conversations and copies of documents. It sure was career-ending stuff for a whole lot of people in the Establishment.

'Fuck them,' I said. 'Trev, do it, mate.'

'Roger that. Hold on to your seats, folks. This is going to be massive.'

Trev had tried explaining to me about offshore proxy servers and untraceable IP addresses and a whole lot of boring shit I couldn't follow. I was only interested in results.

And we got them all right.

In less than half an hour the impact was hitting, with the unsourced material erupting forth. The Internet and the media went into meltdown, and the Australian government was following fast.

Me? I needed to find solace in the raw sordidness of sex. Nothing could compare in reminding you of your humanity. No philosophical musing could come close to sex for answering those existential questions.

I made a phone call.

A leafy terrace in Paddington was home to Carmen's well-heeled residence.

I hefted the brass knocker, armed with a cold bottle of Veuve.

She opened the door. She was wearing a translucent, cobalt blue negligée.

She pulled me through the doorway, slamming it closed.

'So, detective, time to investigate my body.'

'Madam, rest assured it will be a seriously thorough investigation. And a very long and hard one.'

'Just how I like it.'

She plunged her tongue into my mouth with more vigour than a Viking entering an English convent.

Time to pillage and plunder, I reckoned.

She rushed me upstairs and we got naked at warp speed.

Carmen gave head like an angel, of the fallen variety.

By the time I had assuaged my desperate base desires an hour later, she'd fallen a lot further.

She lay asleep next to me.

I felt some semblance of calm return to my mind.

Gazza, I thought, rest in peace, brother. You had the last word on those wankers.

A.B. Patterson is an Australian writer who knows first-hand about corruption, power, crime and sex. He was a Detective Sergeant in the Western Australia Police, working in paedophilia and vice, and later a Chief Investigator with the Independent Commission Against Corruption in Sydney.

His multiple award-winning, debut novel, *Harry's World*, introduced readers to the jaded and flawed PI Harry Kenmare. *Harry's Quest* was the sizzling, award-winning sequel in the PI Harry Kenmare series of novels. The third novel, *Harry's Grail*, is a work in progress, due out in 2024.

He has had short stories, all dark and mostly crime, published in various anthologies and magazines, including *Switchblade, Pulp Modern,* and *Econoclash Review.*

His Harry Kenmare short stories, some previously published in the USA in *Switchblade* magazine, were gathered together for the first time in *Harry Kenmare, PI – At Your Service.*

His hard-boiled, gritty, and noir writing style has been likened to that of Raymond Chandler and Ken Bruen. He's a massive fan of both of them.

He is a proud and active member of the Independent Fiction Alliance, believing ardently in the freedom of creative expression.

You can find him at: **www.abpatterson.com.au**, and on social media.

Nathan Hill is an actor, writer, producer and director. Having gained success with his film *The Strange Game of Hyde and Seek* (2004), *Fox Force* (2009) and *Model Behaviour* (2013), his film opened the Australian Film Festival. He is a Shriekfest Finalist and California Film Award Winner. *Revenge of the Gweilo* (2020), in which he acted & directed, won the Indie Gathering International Film Festival, along with a host of others. He has acted in all mediums of the entertainment world, with his debut on the stage playing Peter Pan and his screen debut as a vampire in *Queen of the Damned* (2002). He is currently in production on his latest erotic thriller feature, *Bitter Desire*, and is in post-production on the sci-fi thriller, *Alien Love*. He is the founder and Executive Producer of Nathan Hill Productions. He lives in Melbourne, Australia.

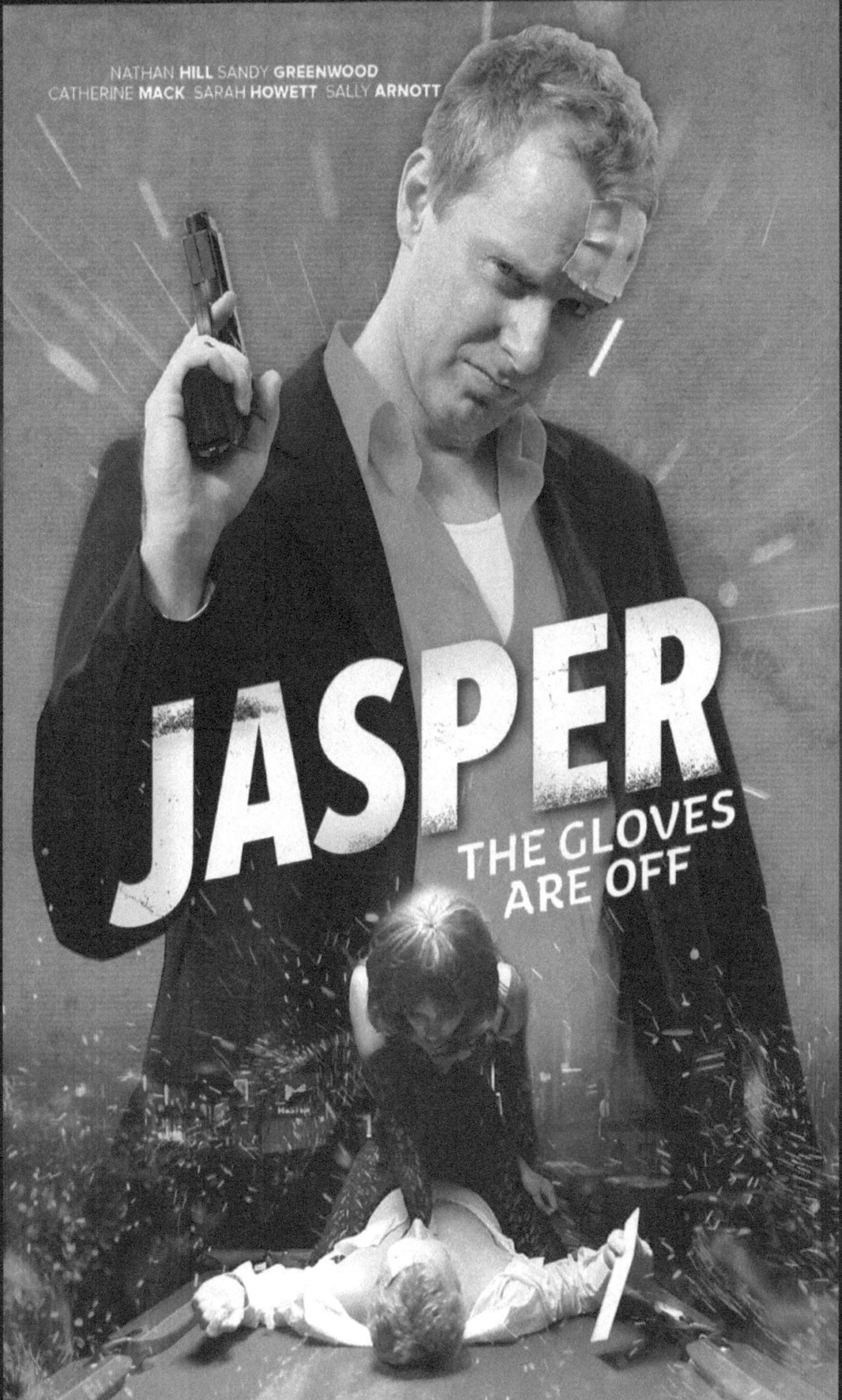
NATHAN HILL SANDY GREENWOOD
CATHERINE MACK SARAH HOWETT SALLY ARNOTT
JASPER
THE GLOVES
ARE OFF

A.B. PATTERSON

NOW AVAILABLE IN PAPERBACK

HARRY KENMARE, PI
AT YOUR SERVICE

PI Harry Kenmare loves gorgeous women, fine wine, and Irish whiskey. And he loves to see justice done. He's old school: results matter, methods don't, and political correctness can go to hell, along with the corrupt Establishment.

L.A. STORIES
TEMPLE OF THE RAT
THE ROACH KING OF PARADISE
LADY TOMAHAWK
1979
SLEAZE
IS KING
CIZAK
RUTHERFORD
MILLER

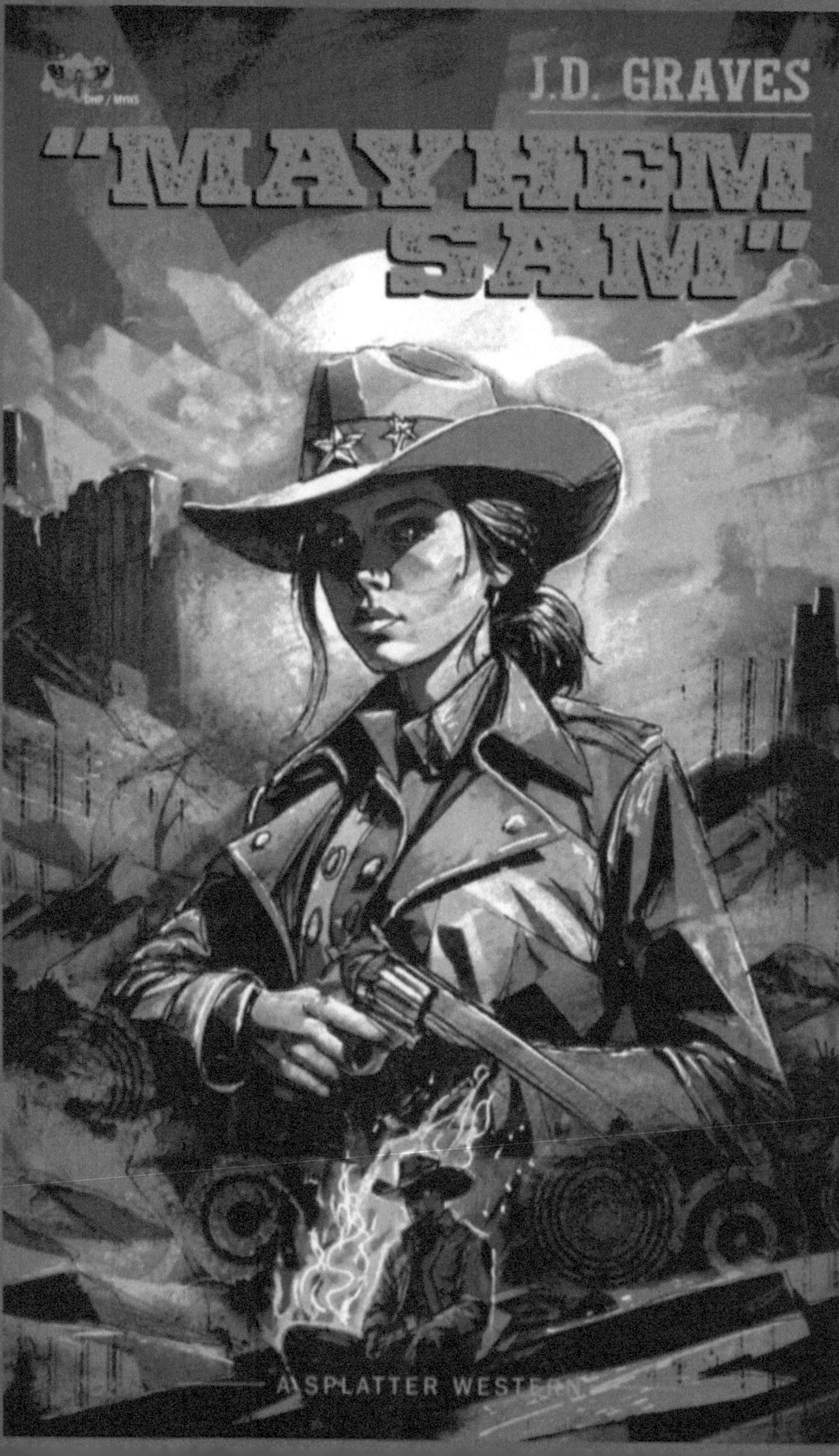
J.D. GRAVES
"MAYHEM SAM"
A SPLATTER WESTERN

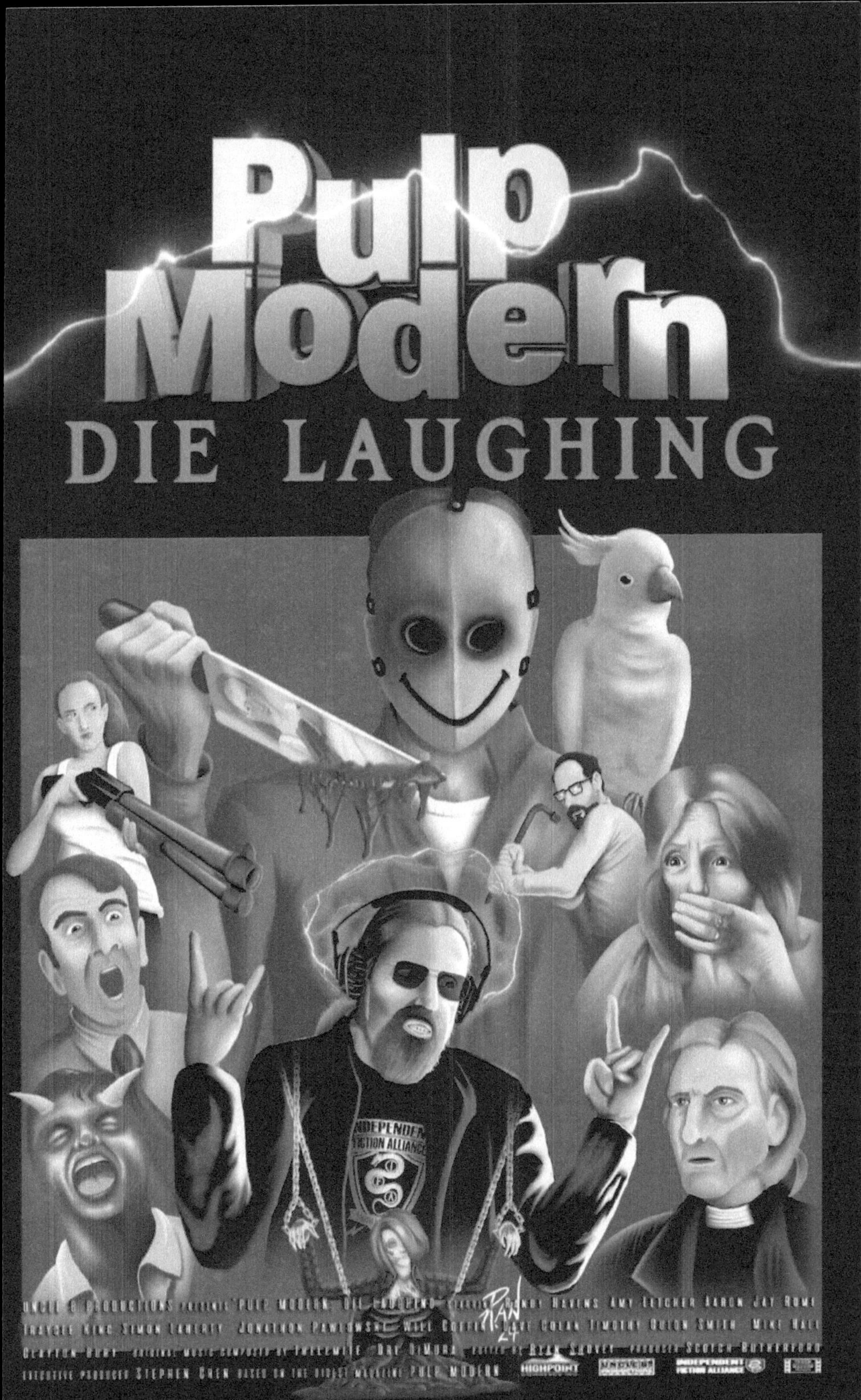
Pulp Modern
DIE LAUGHING
INDEPENDENT FICTION ALLIANCE
HIGHPOINT

www.ingramcontent.com/pod-product-compliance
Lightning Source LLC
Chambersburg PA
CBHW022037170626
46808CB00003B/1244

* 9 7 8 1 9 5 7 0 3 4 5 0 8 *